A DAY LATE

A DAY LATE

CAROLYN DOTY

THE VIKING PRESS / NEW YORK

First published in 1980 by The Viking Press
625 Madison Avenue, New York, N.Y. 10022
Published simultaneously in Canada by
Penguin Books Canada Limited

LIBRARY OF CONGRESS CATALOGING IN PUBLICATION DATA
Doty, Carolyn.
A day late.
I. Title.
PZ4.D697Day   [PS3554.O79]   813'.5'4   79–23581
ISBN 0–670–25923–3

Printed in the United States of America
Set in Old Style #7

ACKNOWLEDGMENTS

Chappell Music Company: From *Just in Time.*
Copyright © 1956 by Betty Comden, Adolph Green
& Jule Styne. Stratford Music Corp., owner. Chappell & Co., Inc. & G. Schirmer, Inc., Administrators of
publication and allied rights. International Copyright Secured. All Rights reserved. Used by permission.

G & W Famous Music Publishing Companies: From
That's Amore by Jack Brooks and Harry Warren.
Copyright © 1953 by Paramount Music Corporation.

Home Run Systems Corp.: From *It Must Be Sunday,* by Phoebe Snow.

United Artists Music Publishing Group, Inc.: From
The Gang That Sang 'Heart of My Heart' by Ben
Ryan. Copyright © 1926, renewed 1954 Robbins
Music Corporation. Used by permission.

TO WILLIAM DOTY,
ANNE RICE,
AND LEONARD BISHOP

PART ONE

Sam Batinovich was on the brink of the Utah-Nevada desert headed into the white hot salt flats. He was not in the racing car of his sometime dreams, not in a silver plane, not in a Cadillac, but in a new Chevrolet station wagon with wood-paneled sides, and it was still not enough.

A piece of circular sun flashed from the windshield of an oncoming car, and he thought this was a hell of a place to be celebrating his forty-first birthday. He drove into the blue shadow of a mountain, and shook his head at the contrast and the adjustment his eyes had to make.

He had difficulty with his concentration. He still listened to thoughts through the strong steady note of pain that had pierced his body and his soul the day the head of neurosurgery had stood before them and said, "Your daughter has an inoperable tumor, hopeless, a month, maybe two, sorry," running the words together, hurrying to get them over. Sam had been aware of Thelma's knees giving way beneath her. He had been unable to catch her before she stumbled against the desk, and the doctor with his damned sanctimonious white jacket had straightened her up and Sam wanted to yell, *Julianna, fourteen and dying*. The shrill tone rose in his head, stayed there through the death, and was still present two months later.

August twelfth and seven hundred miles from home. He

had not had his breakfast. His hands were shaking from the pint of warm bourbon he had consumed alone in a motel in Salt Lake City. It was summer, and the ice machine outside his door had clanked when he deposited his quarter, belched up one chunk, then nothing. So he had sat on the bed with a water glass in hand, the bottle on the night stand.

He had watched Johnny Carson interview a blond woman who looked at the camera, smiled, and said she didn't understand the question. Sam had wanted to laugh. Johnny stared at the woman's breasts. She wore a shirt that was slit halfway to the navel and had sequin eyes (one open, one closed) over each nipple. Sam tried to imagine Thelma in a shirt like that, and could not. He thought the woman looked false, like a large doll. Everything about her was too shiny. But he knew that somewhere the woman went to the grocery store, and talked to people, and maybe even cried at sad movies. She was alive and walking around, and the fact that he had never grabbed some sweetie by her sequined breasts was not her fault or Johnny Carson's, but his own. It wasn't as if he were too old.

Sam pulled the station wagon into Cora's Desert Rose Cafe, comfortable with the notion that he was right on schedule. Cora would tell him a good dirty joke to start out the day. He could laugh, wink at her, proposition her, and she would pretend delight and agree. It would be a relief to look into a woman's eyes that were not filled with tears, not red-rimmed and accusatory.

Sam would say, "Listen, sweetheart, it's my birthday." Cora would laugh, slap him on the back, and say, "You stay round here tonight and old Cora'll give you a treat you won't forget," and by damn, he just might do it.

His hands were clammy on the steering wheel, and he turned off the ignition and swore at the heat as he opened the station wagon door. He could imagine himself with a big-breasted girl with long blond hair and a tee shirt open to the waist. He would reach inside and warm one damp hand on her breast. The sequin eyes would wink, and by God, he would wink back.

Sam had been on the same run for eleven years. Sam Batinovich, industrial cleaner salesman. Oakland to Eugene, Oregon, across through Bend and Burns to Twin Falls, Idaho, down to Salt Lake City and across the desert home. Sam liked the openness, and he liked to drive alone. He listened to the radio when he could get a station, and he sang old songs to himself when he could not. Sam Batinovich, who grew up in Montana, the high country where it was almost never hot, stepped out into the early morning heat of the edge of the desert.

He glanced up at the sign. A ribbon of trembling pink neon outlined a rosebud. The Desert Rose Cafe. Sam pulled at the spring-held screen door.

"Put the door in the hole," Cora would yell at him, and then she would laugh.

"It's my birthday," Sam would say. "I'm twenty-one." He would not tell her his daughter had died, that was why it had been so long since his last trip. He would not tell her about the shrill tone of pain in his head. He wanted to laugh. He wanted to remember the words to those old songs. Johnny Carson laughed, tapped his pencil, stared at the woman's breasts, blinked his eyes. Sequin eyes, raising and lowering with each nervous breath the blonde took, with each shift of her shoulders.

Cora, with her red hair piled high on her head in shiny bubble curls, stood with her back to him, waiting on two men in the corner booth. Her brother, Jimmy, was pouring coffee for a driver who was hunched over the counter. Cora did not see Sam.

He slid onto a stool at the end of the counter. It was the

only vacant seat. He watched Cora, ready to signal her the minute she turned around.

"I just can't see myself being a father to some other guy's kid," the man next to him said. "I mean, the first time the kid does something wrong and I correct him, the old lady's going to get all over me." He spoke to a meek-looking man with thinning blond hair.

Cora chatted casually with the men in the booth, her hand on her hip. She threw back her head and laughed, and Sam thought she was getting hippier. She was still pretty thin, but her uniform was tighter around the butt than it had been before. He wished she would hurry.

Jimmy waved the coffee pot in a salute to Sam and started toward him. The driver coughed and slapped a quarter on the counter with a crack. A salesman in a pale blue suit reached for his briefcase and signaled for his check.

Cora had gone into the kitchen without noticing Sam. *It's my birthday* waited to be said and there was no one to say it to, certainly not Jimmy, who placed a rattling cup and saucer in front of Sam.

"Tell your gorgeous sister that the man in her life is here," Sam said to Jimmy.

The man next to Sam turned to look at him. The man wore a blue cotton shirt open to the middle of his chest. His face was tanned and heavily lined, contrasting with the youthful body and the thick brown hair. Around his neck he wore a chain with a liquid-silver charm. The charm was the same color as the stubble on his face. Sam rubbed his hand over his own chin. He had remembered to shave.

"Sure thing, Sam," Jimmy said as he pushed a greasy plastic menu across the counter.

"A buddy of mine married a doctor's wife once. She had

three kids. Got four hundred a month child support and another four hundred alimony. That's why the guy married her. He lasted three years. Hardest money he ever earned." The man with the silver chain shook his head. "I just can't see myself . . ."

"Well, hello, handsome," Cora said, leaning a thin arm on the counter. "I was about to list you as a missing person. Either that or a ptomaine victim." She laughed. "Got to watch the dives you eat in, honey." She wore a pink uniform with a ruffled handkerchief pinned to her front pocket. She smoked two packages of Chesterfields a day, and kept her fingernails polished with some pearly stuff. She wore red lipstick and smooth pink rouge on her cheeks. She was shiny in her own way, Sam thought. But nice.

"Who you calling *handsome*?" the man with the silver chain around his neck asked.

"Certainly not you," she said, pouring coffee into Sam's cup. "You're just an overgrown paperboy."

"Is that any way to talk about a hardworking man?" His voice was low, with a whiskey edge to it.

The small man with the thinning hair laughed nervously.

"If Jenny Perkins had any sense," Cora went on, the coffee pot poised in her hand, "she'd stay clean away from you."

"That's a jealous woman speaking," the man with the chain said.

"You don't have anything I want, honey," Cora laughed as she fussed with one of the red curls.

"I was about to take my business elsewhere," she said, turning back to Sam. "I'm damned near out of everything."

"I've got plenty of supplies in the car," Sam said. "Get me something to eat, then I'll check your stock."

She took her notebook out of her apron pocket. "How's the family?" she asked, as Sam studied the menu. The words blurred in front of his eyes. He wanted to tell her, but he couldn't do it then.

"I mean, the first sign of trouble and that kid is going to look me straight in the face and say 'You're not my old man.' "

"Eggs over, hard, sausage," Sam said. "And a glass of V-8 juice."

While he waited, he stared into his coffee cup and saw Julianna withering against the white sheets of the hospital bed. He saw her hair, flat and falling out, her face shrinking like a raisin, age crushing her in speeded-up time. Smaller and smaller, older and older, time compressed by some vicious camera that watched, then ran faster—the kind they used to photograph flowers opening and closing. That was what happened to people. Only they died fast, before your eyes like that, and Sam was sick to his stomach at the thought of it all.

Sam scowled; he could feel the tightness in his face. Jimmy poured more coffee into Sam's cup. Sam saw an open sore on the side of Jimmy's neck. Ingrown hair, something festering.

"Got to get those papers in the racks," the man with the silver chain said, as he reached in his pocket for change.

A new waitress, a girl with curly brown hair, and a wide innocent face, smiled at Sam as she passed by with two plates of French toast.

"You're just as gorgeous as ever," Sam said to Cora as she put his breakfast in front of him, but his eyes moved to the young girl who was drawing a glass of milk from the machine.

"Sex and hormone shots," Cora grinned, winking at him. "The wonders of medical science."

Wonders. He had railed at the doctors as Julianna died.

He had cursed them to Thelma. And all the time, she had looked at him. She knew. He could see it in her trembling eyes.

Julianna says she has headaches all the time.

You're making that kid into a hypochondriac.

I don't think it's a good idea to let things go.

She's just a kid. You're dragging her into some doctor's office six times a month. If there was something wrong, they'd find it.

The doctors said it wouldn't have mattered, but the accusations were there, winding and twisting about with the shrill note of pain. Thelma did not believe.

The rage when Julianna had died. His helplessness. And Thelma looking at him as if he was somehow supposed to fix it. Like it was a stopped-up sink, or a stuck cupboard door. Make it right. Undo it. He had wished for a moment that he'd had his gun. He could have run through the halls, those damned pale green halls with the pictures of sunflowers evenly placed. Where even the footsteps sounded like dying. He could have lined up the doctors who were supposed to have saved his daughter, and he would have shot each one of them in the neck. A small oozing hole, like the one on Jimmy's neck. What was a man supposed to do?

"Well, I'm just going to have to tell her it's no soap," the man with the chain said as he stood up from the counter.

The man with the thinning hair said, "I guess so," although he did not sound convinced.

Sam ate his breakfast. He thought about the cows that stared at him as he sighted the gun on a beer can propped up on a fence post. He weighted the empty cans down with rocks so they would not blow over. Perfect targets. It was the noise, the loud retort of the pistol, that helped him the most. It drowned out the siren in his head.

He wiped his hands on the napkin and took one last drink of the ice water. It was a long desolate trip home, and he was not certain he wanted to go. Thelma was trying so hard to keep busy, and it made it difficult for him to keep up the anger. He could not imagine where he would be without it. He thought he might collapse and die.

"Let's you and me go into the back room, honey," Cora said. "We need to be alone." She laughed as if she had said those very words hundreds of times.

"You're all talk," he said, getting up from the stool.

In the storeroom, Cora shook a cigarette from the pack and lit it. She leaned against the shelves while Sam made notations in an order book.

"Where have you been, Sam?" she asked, blowing a straight stream of smoke in his direction.

"Had some troubles at home," he said, marking her down for four gallons of concentrated floor cleaner. He was afraid to look at her, afraid of what she might see.

"Sorry to hear that." Her voice was soft and sympathetic. Cora was not the type to ask what went wrong. Sam knew that.

"By the way," he said, counting the boxes of concentrated window cleaner, "today's my birthday. You going to give me a kiss?" He paused. The words sounded more strained than he had intended. "Or something . . ."

She laughed and moved toward him. She reached up and kissed him lightly on the cheek. "I didn't know you were so sentimental, Sam," she smiled and took one of his hands.

"You sure do smell good," he said, squeezing her hand.

"It's my one real luxury, honey," she said. "Joy perfume. Hundred bucks an ounce."

"It's worth every penny," he said as he put his pencil in his pocket.

As he unloaded the cartons of cleaner that Cora needed, the smell of the perfume lingered in his mind. He wondered if the woman with the sequin shirt had ever heard of Joy perfume. Cora seemed all soft where the shiny woman was hard. And Thelma. If he bought her some perfume, would it help? She seemed so fragile, as if the death had taken some vital fluid from behind her eyes. She tried to be cheerful, and that made it worse. He was afraid to look at her too closely for fear he would see that she, too, was dying.

It was nearly eight and more people were coming into the cafe. Summer travelers, August shirts, dark glasses. A woman whose arms were a mass of freckles carried a straw purse that was decorated with plastic flowers and shells. A sulky looking man with shaking hands was too pale for the end of a vacation. A young woman laughed. A solitary man in a business suit nursed his coffee, the early morning blues. The new waitress smiled shyly at a cowboy who was seated at the counter. The man with the briefcase was long gone.

Cora signed the order and handed it to Sam. At the back door, he stopped and turned to her.

"My Julianna died two months ago," he said. "Cancer. She died on her fifteenth birthday."

Cora's hand rose to her mouth. "Oh, Sam," she murmured.

He looked at his shoes, then past Cora's pain-filled eyes to the sun-blinded desert.

"I know," he said.

He knew she watched him as he unlocked the door of the station wagon. He would join the summer caravan across Nevada, westward. He waved at Cora from behind the wheel.

She hadn't had time to tell him a single joke.

Between Cora's Cafe and Wendover, Nevada, stretches one of the most unusual geographical areas in the United States. The salt flats. White and crystalline, blazing in the daylight, shimmering blue in the moonlight, and looking snow spread. Sam had driven the wide sweeping highway so many times he could do so without concentrating. He looked at the words spelled out with stones in the salt. FUCK YOU. STICK IT. Then innocently enough, THE ELMER C. PETERSON FAMILY WAS HERE.

Sam had the impulse to stop the station wagon and gather some stones and spell into the salt flats, JULIANNA BATINOVICH. He began to scan the white surface for rocks. He could not see enough. Did the scribes of the desert bring their own stones with them? From the canyons, from the quarries? He could steal someone else's words. He could remove a few FUCK YOU's, a few initials, and he could make a monument. He put his hand to his forehead. He could feel beads of perspiration though the air conditioner hummed away. He could gather up those dirty words and make her lovely name. Julianna. She would look at him with eyes frosted over with pain and faintly nod.

How damned hard it was to pretend. Didn't he want, just once, to give himself over. He had known from the minute the flat-faced doctor spoke that Julianna would die. He would like to have said it, just once, right out in the open. Dammit, she's going to die; I feel it in my bones and she knows it, too, so why are we telling all these lies to each other?

He reached for the radio knob. He was tired of thinking about it. He looked at the distant mountains that rimmed pale blue and pink, far away. Thelma was expecting him home tomorrow. She would have a dinner for his birthday.

What does it matter it's a day late, she would say. What does it matter?

He busied his mind with trivia. He was out of clean socks and handkerchiefs and had only one pair of shorts left. He listened to the radio, to dreamy songs that could put a person to sleep at the wheel and wished they would play something more lively.

He sang along with a mournful version of "Heart of My Heart."

"I love that melody," his voice boomed into the loneliness.

> *"Heart of my heart, brings back a memory.*
> *When we were kids . . ."*

He laughed.

> *"On the corner of the street . . ."*

It seemed ludicrous to be singing, and he turned off the radio.

Sam had neglected to use the men's room at the Desert Rose. Ahead was the observation point outside Wendover. Small square brick buildings stood out against the flatness like a child's forgotten building blocks. There was a platform raised high, a concrete curving ramp to allow the tourists to survey the salt flats and the Bonneville Speedway.

It was nearly ten o'clock in the morning.

It'll be hotter than hell out there, he thought, and he turned into the parking lot at the observation point. Glancing at his watch, he was suddenly annoyed with his schedule, with the necessity of it. He wished they had a target set up on the salt flats. He would take his pistol from the glove compartment and a full clip and blast the hell out of a bull's-eye. He would drown out the pain, and the damned singsongy melody that circled it.

It was a shame to have extra time when others had no time at all.

Katy Daniels rested her forehead on the wall of the toilet stall and closed her eyes. She pressed the button on the floor and a loud rush of water violently cleansed the bowl.

"Did someone throw up?" a little girl asked.

"Sssh," a woman said.

Katy felt the tears of embarrassment in her eyes. The little girl peeked under the door. The ruffle of Katy's long skirt was visible as well as her sandaled feet.

"Stop that," the woman said, "stop it right now."

"Who is that?" asked the child.

"Shush," replied the woman.

Katy Daniels was on her way home. Home to the rhododendron- and azalea-covered hills of Berkeley. Home to the large house with the leaded glass windows and French doors that opened out into the garden. Home to a mother who wrote poetry, to a father whose medical practice consisted primarily of lectures and administrative duties, to a grandmother who wore batik kaftans and talked about Zen, and to two pesty younger brothers.

And Katy had a surprise for them all. Pretty Katy who had gone away to Colorado to find herself had found someone else instead. Kurt Edwards, father of her unborn child. He mysteriously vanished the day after she told him the news, and he left no forwarding address.

Katy flushed the toilet again. The words of explanation planned for her parents changed from one moment to the next. Sometimes she cried and begged forgiveness. Sometimes she accused them. "You never should have let me go. You didn't care enough about me."

"Why is that girl sick?" the child asked.

Oh, please go away, Katy thought. She heard the whispers, but could not distinguish the words. She heard the sound of rubber-soled shoes on the concrete floor. Then the woman and child were gone.

Katy unlatched the door and caught sight of her reflection in the mirror. Although she was a little pale, she certainly did not look as ill as she felt. She went to the basin and washed her face with a paper towel. She wiped around her neck, across her shoulders. Although the toweling was rough, the water was soothing. She lifted the hem of her long skirt and looked at her feet. She would wash them, too. A powdered-soap and paper-towel bath. When she finished, she dusted her sandals with the wet towel. She searched her backpack for toothbrush and paste, and for a clean tee shirt. She wanted to get a good ride this time, someone who would take her the rest of the way. She chose a white shirt with a cotton lace inset in the front.

Then she studied her face in the mirror and rubbed some color into her cheeks. On Katy's sixteenth birthday, her grandmother had said to her, "Oh, you're such a pretty girl. You'll have to work extra hard to be a good person." Katy had concentrated on her grandmother's coral lipstick, the lipstick that bled into the fine age lines around her mouth. She remembered that and the feel of her grandmother's hand on her cheek.

She brushed her long brown hair until it was shiny, and she straightened the cotton skirt.

They hadn't really asked her if she wanted to go. They'd had a family council and decided that it would be good for her to get away. They didn't want to be overly protective. They didn't want to stifle her as a person. They didn't want her to resent them later. They didn't want to be called "conservative."

A middle-aged woman with freckled arms opened the door to the restroom and smiled at Katy. She carried a straw purse decorated with plastic flowers and shells.

Katy, with her pack on her shoulder, stepped out into the sunlight. Several automobiles, campers, three motor homes, and two station wagons were parked at the observation point. Katy began checking the license plates. New Jersey. Could be going either direction. California, California, Utah. One of the California cars had three small children climbing about in the back seat, and Katy thought they probably would not want to add her. Families were not a good bet.

At the end of the first row was a white station wagon with wooden sides. Katy could see cartons of something in the back, but the front seat was remarkably clean. One suitcase, a jacket on a hanger. A wagon this new was certain to have air conditioning. California. She leaned her pack against the front bumper of the car. She took her sunglasses from her purse and began to look for the owner of the station wagon. Could she guess? A man in a light blue suit came out of the restroom, but he got into a green car. A man stood on the observation platform looking out over the salt flats, but he seemed to have a little girl with him. She could not see anyone else who looked like a salesman.

She rested her hip against the car to wait. He must be in the restroom. He had to be somewhere. And, she thought, if something looks better, I can always check it out from here. She folded her arms and watched the man on the observation deck. The hot sun, for the moment, felt good on her arms.

Sam stood on the grating at the top of the platform and looked out onto the empty speedway. He squinted even though he wore dark glasses. The white was brilliant, perilous to look at and devastating in its concept. It raced with itself because of the emptiness, interlocking dazzling speed with surface. Sam's eyes slid freely along, and he gripped the railing and leaned forward. A girl about four years old ran up and down the ramp, her tennis shoes slapping the concrete, her child giggles rattling in the blue-white air.

Sam's arms were muscular with thick black hair. He played softball once in a while, bowled some, fished a little, but it was the lifting of the boxes of industrial concentrate that kept him in shape. Since it was his job, he did not think of it as exercise. He had thick curly dark hair with a few strands of gray. He did not worry about baldness. His own father had died with a full head of black hair, and his grandfather had looked like a young man when he was seventy. Sam's olive skin had weathered the years nicely, and his sisters commented that he had become more handsome than ever.

"Yes," Thelma had said, "hasn't he." She had smiled shyly at Sam. But that was before. Thelma with dark eyelashes, a secret smile.

Sam's Yugoslavian parentage gave him strength and health. If he had not been scowling intensely at the empty speedway, one might have mistaken him for a happy-go-lucky man. The muscles in his forearms stood out as he gripped the railing.

"Where are the racing cars?" a little boy asked.

"There aren't any races today," the boy's mother replied.

"Then why are we looking? What are we looking at?"

"The scenery. Can't you look at the mountains or something?"

Sam was amused. Why couldn't he just look at the scenery, too?

The little girl running up and down the ramp bumped his leg. She wore a yellow sunsuit, and on her shoulders were peeling patches of pink skin. He wanted to touch her small hand, but he did not. He smiled, remembering Julianna. Three or four years old, running down the green grassy knolls at the park. Short legs churning, giggling, running at a flock of pigeons, arms outstretched. She thought it was possible to catch a bird in her hand. Little girls ran down hills as fast as they could and never thought they would fall.

Was it courage or just a lack of sense?

"Hi," he said to the child, squatting down to look into her round blue eyes. Her face was red from running, and she giggled at him and ran away. He watched her go to a woman who had a camera sighted toward the desert. The child pulled at the woman's flowered shorts.

"That man, see that man. He talked to me. See."

Sam stood and stared at the mother and daughter. The woman frowned. She bent down and said stern words. Warnings. Sam knew from her expression. Don't talk to strangers. Never take anything from a stranger. He

thought he could remember saying those very words to
Julianna.

He wanted to grab the woman by her thin arm and yell
at her. *I am a parent, too, lady, and don't you look at me
that way.*

He started down the ramp. He was a businessman. Get
on the road. He had to see Johnny Leone in Elko. He
should say hello to Kristo in Winnemucca. Sam looked
after his customers. They were people who kept their
establishments clean.

Sam's products were the strongest concentrates around.
Klean-Away Kleaners were developed by Mr. Armadine
Pencimil of Emeryville, California, and he still mixed the
batches himself. Mr. Pencimil was a tiny quiet man, and
Julianna had imagined he was a wizard. "He makes
damned good cleaner," Sam had told her. "That makes
him kind of a wizard."

Maybe he would get into Wells early and take a spin in
the flat pink whorehouse by the railroad tracks. He needed
to put his arms around a woman who did not recognize
him. A woman with a tee shirt with sequin eyes. He
laughed. He couldn't get that tee shirt out of his mind.

A young woman leaned against the front of his station
wagon. She did not seem to see him coming. She was looking at her feet. There was a pack on the ground beside
her. She was thin, too thin, Sam thought. Her hair fell
down past her shoulders, hiding part of her face.

God, it was hot, he thought, looking up at the sky. A
thunderstorm would be nice. Cool the desert down
quickly. Thunderclouds rolling across the flats. Maybe
there was a slight smell of it in the air.

He expected the girl to move as he neared the car. Instead, she merely straightened and looked at him. He saw
his reflection in her mirror dark glasses, his body gro-

tesquely distorted, but as clear as a photograph, staring back at him, double.

"Is this your station wagon?" Katy asked politely.

"Yes," Sam replied. "It sure is. Only had it a month now."

"I see you're from Albany. The license plate holder," she explained. "It says Albany."

He thought she must be a pretty girl, but he could not tell without seeing her eyes. She seemed young, under twenty.

"Right. I live in Albany." He could not connect the questions to the girl who must be waiting for someone. Too young to be alone.

Katy cleared her throat. "I need a ride home to Berkeley, and since Albany's so close, I thought maybe I could ride with you."

Sam studied her without seeing her, the twin images of himself in her glasses annoying him. He did not take riders. He could not sing in the car with someone sitting next to him, not even Thelma; though once, a long time ago, they had sung all the way to Montana, or so it seemed. Julianna in the back seat clapping her hands to "Four and twenty blackbirds . . ." and "Oh, Suzanna . . ."

But then, he did not feel like singing anyway.

"Where exactly do you live in Berkeley?" he asked.

"On the Arlington," she said. "Almost into Kensington."

Sam knew the tree-lined street filled with large expensive homes. Why would someone who lived there be hitchhiking?

"Do you live with your parents?" he asked.

She began to rub her hands together nervously. He wondered if the eyes behind the glasses were pleading.

"Yes," she said, "and my grandmother, two brothers." She added softly, "My father's a doctor."

Something confusingly white went through Sam's mind. A numbness.

"I didn't have enough money for the bus," Katy added, "and I wanted to surprise them."

Sam steadied himself against the car and felt the searing heat on his palm.

"What's your father's name?" he asked.

"Daniels," Katy said. "My name is Katy."

Daniels. Sam did not recognize it. He frowned. "If you were my daughter, I wouldn't let you travel by yourself."

"I'm older than I look."

"That doesn't matter. You aren't old enough."

"I've been to Colorado," she said, as if that were the explanation.

"I'm a salesman," Sam said. "I have to make stops along the way."

"I'm not in any hurry."

"I don't expect to get home until tomorrow."

"Oh," she said. She looked down at her hands.

For some reason, perhaps it was the flicker of eyelashes that he saw through the glasses, he thought she might be going to cry.

He extended his hand. "Sam Batinovich," he said. "Ba-*tin*-o-vich. I can take you as far as Reno." His words surprised him.

She put a small damp hand into his. "Thank you," she said, and her mouth seemed to tremble with the smile.

Julianna should be alive and well and waiting for him to come home. Instead, this girl stood before him. She bent to pick up her pack, and Sam could see that she did not wear a brassiere, but that her breasts were very small.

The numbness spread, then broke, and Sam was close to

tears at the sight of the girl. He bent to take the pack from her. He unlocked the door and placed the pack on top of a half empty box of concentrate.

"You better sit up front," he said calmly. "Cooler, right in front of the air conditioner." He still did not smile.

Katy hesitated a moment, as if reconsidering, then said, "Thanks."

Sam sat behind the wheel and leaned across to open the door for Katy. Looking sideways at the girl, he thought he would not bother to tell Thelma about this. The girl stared straight ahead as Sam slipped the gear into reverse and prepared to back out of the parking space.

"How old are you?" he asked.

"Seventeen," Katy said. "I graduated from high school in January."

He eased the station wagon onto the highway, merging with the caravan heading west. Because of the color, the station wagon was soon lost to the eye, becoming only a metallic glare, a smaller, less defined member of the procession.

The air conditioner was working. The girl sighed, sucking the cool air in through her mouth. She leaned her head against the seat, and Sam resisted an impulse to tell her to sit up straight, not to slump down like that. Would ruin her spine.

"What kind of a doctor is your father?" Sam asked.

"He's an endocrinologist," Katy answered. "Mostly he does research now."

"He works with glands, then," Sam said. He twisted the gold band on his finger. Something, a grain of sand or sugar, was lodged between the metal and the skin.

"He's gone a lot," Katy said. "He gives papers and speeches all over the world."

"He must do pretty well for you to live in one of those big houses."

"I don't think it makes all that much difference what kind of a house a person lives in."

Sam's hands tightened on the steering wheel. He stared ahead at the road. WENDOVER 1 MILE. He bit his lip, shook his head. The heat reflected from the window onto his face.

"It's easy for the ones that live in the big houses to make statements like that," he said.

He had talked with Kristo about that, about those people who had always had money. Kristo, whose parents came from Greece. Sam, whose father came from Yugoslavia. "It's the old country heritage, Sam. We've got it coursing around in our veins and it still makes us different." Kristo said this from the position of success, wearing an expensive suit, drinking the finest Scotch. Sam and Thelma had gone to Hawaii a year ago, before the illness began. Kristo wanted to go to Greece, and it all seemed possible.

"What I mean," Katy said, "is that I think the people who live in the houses are more important than the houses themselves."

"You've never had to live in a dump," Sam said.

He was immediately sorry. He would never have said such a thing to Julianna, and he would have been angry with anyone who snapped at her the way he had just done to Katy. Besides, he hadn't lived in such bad places himself. He grew up in a frame farmhouse edged by lush green meadow, ringed by the highland pines and blue spruce. The house stood tall and narrow in the middle of the yard, the roof pitched steep so the heavy Montana snow would slide off into mounds that came over the windowsills, sealing away the light. The clothesline stretched from the back porch to an old apple tree near the pump. In summer, deep purple violets grew in the shadowed places near the house. In winter, they were buried under sliding snow. Sam's mother had worn violets pinned in a tidy bunch on her breast. The sweet scent of violets, confounding his senses, mixing with the Sunday dinner smells, mixing him up in time, the memory too fragile to hold. His mother had always seemed old, and he was afraid for Thelma.

Sam shook his head. No one wore violets nowadays. He could not remember the last time he had seen a bunch of violets. Thelma had a few African ones around the house, thick fuzzy leaves and tight plastic baskets. Not the same.

"No one wears violets anymore," he whispered.

Katy turned to him. She looked puzzled.

Visions of wild violets. He blinked. Did they blow across the sand-scarred road that led into Wendover? Why was he seeing them today? He moved his hand across his forehead, feeling his damp skin. Cora wore a handkerchief with bright purple violets embroidered in the corner. Cora standing in the doorway waving good-bye. That was it! He was relieved to have found the connection. His mother, with the small fine-stemmed bunch of violets pinned to her breast, was dead and buried. He shook away memories of snow.

Would Julianna have recognized a real violet? A wild one? Had he walked with her when she was small, talking and pointing, explaining? Had he been gentle? They had watched the big bear at the zoo running in his wheel. Gentle, yes. Laughing.

"I'm sorry," Sam said. "I happened to remember that when I was a kid, wild violets grew in our yard. That's all." All the talk about houses and homes.

"Aren't violets supposed to be bad luck?" Katy asked.

Sam laughed. He tipped back his head, feeling his skin stretch and pain against his neck and skull.

"Maybe so," he laughed again. He looked at the approaching main street of Wendover with gratitude. Motels, stores, service stations.

"My mother has some flowers," Katy said, "some little ones called violas, I think. They must be close to the same kind of . . ."

"My mother wore them to church. Guess she didn't think they were bad luck. You wouldn't wear 'bad luck' to a church." He laughed again though he knew there was nothing funny about the conversation.

Sam slowed down. "Have to watch the limit in these towns," he said. "Not as bad as it used to be, but some places supported the community treasury by picking up the tourists. Idaho was the worst. Out of nowhere, the limit would drop down to nothing, and the next thing you knew, there was a cop in back of you." He thought he seemed to be rambling. "Of course, I'd traveled the roads enough that I didn't fall into the traps."

"My little brother has already had his license suspended," Kathy said. "He wrecked my mother's car."

"I'll bet your father was unhappy about that."

"He was out of town. Anyway, it wasn't his car."

"Hell, I'll bet he paid for it."

"I think my grandmother bought it for my mother."

Sam groaned. "The point is—someone paid for it. Right?"

"My grandmother has a lot of money."

"Enough to throw away?"

They passed the pink stucco motels, the crowded service stations, the wind-faded sun-bleached pastels. Even the few trees blew pale in the breeze. Wendover. Flat, dust-covered against the white light of the desert sun.

"What a place to gain an hour," he said, winding his watch backwards from ten-twenty to nine-twenty. Katy looked confused. "The time zone," he added. "This is where we change."

He drove along the street at twenty-five. Violets in the corner of the yard, violets in the corner of a ruffled handkerchief, violets springing from the soft brown soil of a new grave. He leaned back against the seat, straightening his arms. He was stiff, and he moved his shoulders trying to loosen up. The girl quietly chewed a cracker. He thought of crumbs in his new car, then squinted at his pettiness.

Someone paid. Surely she should be able to see that.

"I guess you've been through here a lot," Katy said.

"Right," Sam answered. He passed the casino with the huge cowboy sign that lured gamblers, beckoning with an electronic arm.

"Do you ever stop and gamble?" she asked.

"No. Too smart for that." He cleared his throat.

RESUME SPEED, the sign read. The words blurred before Sam's eyes.

"If you don't gamble, how do you ever win?" she asked.

"You don't know much about gambling," he snapped.

She was quiet. She looked out the side window as if she were afraid to see him.

"Listen," he said, his voice low in his throat, rasping against the sound of the engine. "I . . ."

He started to tell her that his daughter had died. The words were there. Listen, you be nice to me, young lady, don't be smart with me. I know some things you don't. My daughter died. Two months. Be quiet. You don't know anything.

But he could not say the words. He searched the

thinning landscape. He let his eyes wander over the desert as he looked to the west. Good-bye to Wendover, Nevada, and the spot in the universe credited with the development of the atomic bomb. Sam thought of the newsreels of the mushroom cloud, the rolling black and pink, gold and orange clouds. He was ashamed to think it beautiful, and he wished he had seen one. Just a test, not the real killing thing. He had wanted to be somewhere safe and see an explosion.

"I'm sorry," he said. "I'm out of sorts today."

Kathy closed her eyes. "Okay," she said.

A minor explosion in the vast Nevada desert. If he were to tell her about Julianna, she would feel sad. He settled more comfortably behind the steering wheel. He wished for a cigarette for the first time in months. He wanted her to know that he was an interesting man.

"You know," he said, "during the Bicentennial, they had covered wagons going right along this road. It's the pioneer route to California." Small wagons and dusty clomping horses, minuscule in the landscape, unheard above the roar of the traffic.

Several Last Chances passed through Sam's field of vision. Last chance for food, gas, water, oil. The electronic cowboy waved good-bye.

Katy turned to look back at Wendover and cleared her throat. "Would you mind if I went to sleep?" she asked.

"Go ahead. Long damned trip across this state." There were outposts before them. Wells, Elko, Winnemucca.

She seemed to be trying to be nice, to be polite. He glanced across at her thin arms and the attitude in his stomach changed. He took a deep breath. Trouble like that, he did not need. Not today, not any day. He was a sensible man. This girl was young and pretty and innocent, like the new waitress at Cora's Cafe. She wasn't a big-breasted blonde from the Johnny Carson show with nights of experience running on until it did not matter.

He wished he had a cigarette and a bottle of beer. Anything that would make him forget his daughter's death.

Katy leaned back against the seat and closed her eyes. She shifted about, trying to get comfortable. She scratched her leg, then her elbow. She put her hand on her stomach to calm what felt like small stones moving about. Sam seemed nervous, uncomfortable with her. Although she was not sleepy, she thought he seemed to feel obligated to talk with her as long as she was awake. And then when they did talk, even about her family, he jumped on everything she said.

But then, she supposed Sam probably wouldn't like her mother much. He would think she was pretty; Theoflora Daniels was certainly that. And then she spoke, Katy thought, in that breathy poetic way. She sounded like her name. Nothing really upset her. "In the larger scheme of things," she was wont to say, "this will be but a flicker. . . ." Katy could see her mother brushing her thick black hair back away from her face, pressing her fingers to her cheekbones.

Is that what her mother was going to say when Katy told her the news? A flicker.

Without opening her eyes, and almost in imitation of her mother, Katy brushed a strand of hair away from her face. The air was cool, and she was not as queasy as she had been before.

Sam was a strange man. He wasn't nearly as old as she

had originally thought. He was younger than her father. She doubted Sam would care much for him either. Oh, he was pleasant enough. Just preoccupied. Sam wouldn't like to be ignored that way, Katy thought. He seemed to listen to everything, every sound. What would they have to talk about? Melvin and Theoflora Daniels talked about the mind, about creativity, about intellectual matters. Katy had never seen her father loudly angry, or her mother cry. They had a method for dealing with situations, and it was called *reason*. Her friends called her mother "beautiful," and "nice"; her father "distinguished," and "smart."

Sam, Katy thought, was handsome in a rather old-fashioned way. He did not wear his hair to his shoulders, or a necklace of any kind. Albany. He was, she decided, a conservative. His arms were nice, muscular, covered with curly black hair. She wondered what it would be like to make love to him. Love. That was what she thought she had made with Kurt Edwards.

"Didn't you use something?" Kurt had asked when she told him.

"I guess it didn't work." She had been amazed at how quickly her love for him had dissipated. She wasn't even left with that.

She had met Kurt at The Cellar, a concrete box beneath a shopping plaza where the gray walls and floor had flashed purple and red, yellow and orange, in time to the well-amplified rock group that played there. The light reached everyone. Katy had been sitting in the corner, her face blue, then purple, then red, and while she was orange, she could see the young man across the room turning purple. She took a glass of wine, consuming it quickly before the color came around again. The band was yellow and orange and screaming, and she tapped her foot to the heavy rhythm.

She understood it. Underneath the wailing and the

moaning and the high-pitched scream was the basic un-imaginative thumping of the purest mechanical heart. She was alone and homesick.

She could not go back to her room. Janet, her room-mate, was in bed with the tall thin bellhop from the lodge, and Katy had another hour to wait. She could not help but imagine them flailing about in the single bed, long arms and legs, thumping with the same mechanical beat, turning red and yellow and purple. And while Katy smothered in the noise, the waitress, who looked deaf and blank, put a glass of wine before her. Katy clutched the stem, releasing her eyes and ears, tapping her foot, rock-ing her body, wishing there was some way to go home without giving up. She was dizzy. All she could hear was the thumping and when she closed her eyes, she saw Janet and the tall thin boy with a mole right in the middle of his cheek, and she thought he probably had funny patches of hair on his body. Janet really kept me out of trouble, she would tell her parents. She really looked out for me.

Just as she was about to cry, the purple young man sat down across from her and said, "You're Katy, aren't you? I'm a friend of Janet's. She said you might be here."

Dumbly, Katy looked at him, and she wondered if he knew what Janet and the bellhop were doing, and if that's what he wanted to do, too.

Instead, she called to him above the music in a voice pitched high like a cloud. "Yes. Yes, to anything you say." She smiled and toasted him with an empty glass, and she thought he was beautiful, all red and orange that way.

They had danced until Katy's head cleared. They bumped and jostled with the others, the multicolored crowd. They jumped and stomped their feet, and his hands went around her waist and held her upright while she threw back her head and raised her arms straight into the air, shaking her fingers. Her back arched, and he could have kissed her breasts right there, while the colors mixed together, melting in the middle of the room. She wouldn't have minded. The music would have stopped, the silence making them all black and white, and she would have held his head there until all her unquiet sounds had rushed to the surface and flown, releasing her from the tightness at her center. And he would carry her, white like the Snow Queen, to his kingdom.

He did take her outside. And it was still, the snow blue-white and she was freezing with dots of perspiration from the dance shining like ice on her face. She saw him for the first time, real in the moonlight. His hair was sun-streaked blond, smooth across his forehead as if he had been motionless. His beard was combed, warm and dry as if she had been dancing by herself. They stood, soft in down jackets, unable to touch where it mattered.

"I can't go back to my room yet," Katy said without looking at her watch. "Janet has someone there."

"We can go to mine," he said mysteriously. "I live alone."

She thought he might be covered with golden fuzz. Even and unabrasive. His face was tan from winter snow and white lines at his eyes made him seem friendly. She was certain that he smiled. He did not have a mole on his cheek, and he was no longer purple.

And she had loved him from that moment until the day that she told him.

Katy opened her eyes and caught Sam watching her. He blinked and fixed his gaze on the road.

"This is the worst stretch on the whole damned trip," Sam said. He strained to see around the Airstream trailer that glinted like a silver egg in front of them.

In back of them, an IML truck of green and yellow filled the rear window. They seemed to be caught between two much larger blocks.

"Hang on," Sam said, pushing the accelerator to the floor. He swerved out around the trailer, causing Katy to lean forward and grip the arm rest for balance. Cars approached them on the two-lane road; they ran toward them like beads strung on a wire.

As they passed the driver, Katy saw a small old man who drove leaning forward as if peering through a dense fog. His wife, on the seat next to him, leaned at precisely the same angle.

"God damn," Sam growled as he cut in front of the man and his wife, and the oncoming pickup truck whizzed by, moving over enough to allow for the possibility that Sam would not make it by the trailer. The truck kicked up dust in the barrow pit, and the driver made an obscene gesture at Sam as he passed.

Katy put her hand on her stomach.

"Sorry," Sam said. "Sorry about the language. I always seem to get behind these folks on the two-laners." He shook his head. "There aren't many sunflowers," he said, pointing to the edge of the road where a few dark-centered flowers nodded. "The Indians say that means a light winter."

Blue-white snowdrifts in Colorado. Kurt's arm around her waist as they walked. Would he come looking for her?

"By the way," Katy said, anxious to forget, "do you know Mrs. Sarah Maguire that lives in Albany?"

Sam tapped his fingers on the top of the steering wheel. "No," he said, "don't think I do. Where does she live?"

"Portland Avenue, I think," Katy answered.

"No."

"She used to clean house for my mother."

Sam did not respond, and Katy did not notice the new set to his jaw.

"She was really funny. One day she just quit. My mother was sitting in the living room reading a book, and Mrs. Maguire came in and said she wouldn't work for anyone who didn't work right along with her. My mother's felt guilty about it ever since. Isn't that a funny thing to say?"

"I think she had a point. I think people should clean their own houses."

Katy sighed. She seemed to have made him angry again, and she was merely trying to be nice to him, to talk to him. What did he expect her to say?

"There's a dead dog," Katy said, pointing to the side of the road.

"That's a coyote," Sam replied.

"There're a lot of dead things on this road," Katy added.

"Got to feed the magpies."

He did not seem to want to talk about that either. Katy rubbed her hands together and stared out the front window. She scratched underneath one breast. She could not imagine that something was alive below her ribs, something separate from her.

DIVIDED HIGHWAY 1 MILE.

"There's a dead crow," Katy said.

"He should have left the table before the car came," Sam muttered. "Greed killed that bird."

The minute the road divided, Sam pulled into the center lane. Katy wondered, at that moment, whether he had ever made love to anyone as young as she was. She wondered how different he would be from Kurt Edwards.

"That's the problem with you young kids," the doctor who had examined her said, "You can't wait ten minutes for anything." Was Sam slower because he was older? When he wasn't irritated, he seemed nice enough. Patient. She was almost cold from the air conditioner. She thought about his arms again.

"My hell," Sam said, "will you look at that."

A few yards in front of them were two motorcycles pulling small trailers.

Katy sat up in the seat. "They're from New York," she said. "They must have come all the way across the country like that. What a great thing!"

Each white metal trailer had a comet insignia above the license plate. The second motorcycle was driven by a middle-aged man. A woman sat behind him, hanging on around his waist. He wore a red helmet; she wore blue. Katy waved at them, and the woman raised a black-gloved hand to wave back.

"They're old," Katy said, excitedly. "I thought they would be kids. They must be fifty or sixty."

The lead man was alone on his motorcycle. His trailer was loaded, and on top Katy saw an old wooden director chair, the folding kind with a rust canvas seat and back.

"I can't believe it," Katy said, her face full of smiles. "Wouldn't that be fun? To just travel around from campground to campground, go wherever you wanted to go." She leaned forward in delight.

The lead man turned to look at them as they passed. He had a yellow-white bushy mustache and a bulging stomach. He wore a fluorescent orange vest and a helmet. Safety first. To Katy's amazement, Sam grinned and waved at the man.

Katy waved, too, and smiled at the man. What a thing, she thought, to do what they were doing. There was something astonishingly dignified about the people, as if their presence on the road gave them some peculiar under-standing of the universe.

"You should do those things when you're a kid," Sam said. "When you have all that freedom. Or you have to wait."

Katy shivered. Kurt Edwards had taken away her freedom. And Sam wore a wedding ring, probably had children and all that responsibility. She could not imagine her own parents on motorcycles going across the country.

"My grandmother would absolutely love it," she said. "She's such a funny person. A liberated grandmother." Grandmother Meliss in her crazy kaftans and sandals on her weathered old feet.

"There's something about the road," Sam said. He seemed less nervous. "Something about having a new car and a tank full of gas . . ."

Katy looked at him and smiled, in spite of the un-comfortable memory of her condition. She thought he looked back at her with strange lines of tenderness around his mouth.

They came up behind a camper. The back door was decorated with decals of stags, a jumping trout, a picture of Old Faithful. A child's book, a scrapbook. Illustrated. A bear, a pheasant. And a bumper sticker that read, *If this camper's rockin', don't bother knockin'.*

Sam laughed and shook his head.

"Isn't it great," Katy said, "to see all these things?"

"You just have to learn how to look," Sam said. He pulled out around the camper.

The man who was driving wore a straw cowboy hat and he was laughing or singing or telling a joke. His mouth was moving, and he waved his hand and winked at Sam and Katy.

"They look like they're having a good time," Sam said,

and Katy thought his voice had tightened.

"It's like getting to know a whole bunch of people that you'll never talk to," she said. She wondered why she had never noticed travelers before.

She turned and looked back at the camper. Idaho. So far, she had not seen anyone from Colorado.

Katy slept on the way into Wells, or Sam would have pointed out the cat houses down by the railroad tracks. He could have explained the right side of the tracks, and the wrong side. He wanted her to know some things, the way he had wanted to tell Julianna about going up over the Beartooth Pass with his grandfather. He must have told her the story, but he could not remember for certain. Katy stayed in the car while he said hello to two old customers and checked their stock. Next time through, he would have to look for new clients in Wells and Elko. He'd picked up four new ones in Oregon, and three in Idaho. Not a bad trip.

Katy had been so excited about the people on the motorcycles. Like a little girl, like his little girl. The image of the cyclists stayed with him. At first, they reminded him of coolies, pedaling rickshaws. He'd seen pictures of China. But then he decided that in silhouette, dark against the white, they looked like Romans and chariots, drawing toward the sun. Kristo would love to see them. He wondered if Thelma would ever agree to a trip like that. Timid Thelma. But that was, after all, what he had wanted at one time. Pretty Thelma, holding on to his arm.

Sam had gotten over the dismaying sense of arousal he had felt at watching Katy move in her sleep. He had dismissed from his mind the memory of Julianna, poor thin baby, tiny wizened breasts. His own horror had collided with Katy's childlike enthusiasm, and he had survived intact.

As he drove into Elko, Katy stirred and opened her eyes.

"I have to stop here," he said.

Johnny Leone's Restaurant in Elko had served Char-Broiled Steaks and Italian Food for twenty-six years. The venetian blinds that kept the Nevada sun from disturbing the patrons had probably not been dusted more than twice in that time.

Sam held the door open for Katy, and glanced at the windowsills. Corpses of black iridescent houseflies speckled the white. He shook his head.

"Hey, Sam. Long time—no see," Johnny rushed forward, menus in hand, grinning. He was a short thin man, not much taller than Katy, and he had a line of black mustache.

"Well, John, time flies." Sam tried to laugh. "And speaking of flies . . ."

"And who's this sweet-looking young lady, hey?"

Katy looked down at the floor. She did not seem quite awake yet.

The restaurant was dark and after the sun, Sam had trouble seeing. Red hurricane lamps in the middle of each table drew his eyes. Then, as his pupils widened, the people that moved in shadows about the room came into focus.

"This is Katy. And this here's old Johnny Leone, himself." Was he shouting? His voice sounded too loud for his own ears.

"You want a nice little table for two in the corner, hey, Sam?"

Sam was confused. He looked about the room. "Okay, sure, John. I'll look at your stock, see what you need later."

"No hurry, Sam. No siree."

Katy stood, her hands clasped in front of her. She stared straight ahead with a bored expression.

Sam put his hand on her elbow and steered her behind Johnny to a small square table beneath an illuminated Olympia beer sign and sat down. Above her, soundless white flashing water rolled over the neon falls.

"Why don't you bring me some of that dago red you keep in the kitchen, John?" Sam asked.

"Those days, gone," Johnny answered. "Rosa, she's on another peck. Anyway, the old paisano I used to get the real homemade stuff from passed away last March." He shook his head, "I'll bring you a bottle of Chianti."

"Fine," Sam said. He pretended to study the menu though he knew exactly what he wanted. "You better have a big lunch," he said. "We might not stop to eat again."

"I'm not too hungry."

"Well, you eat something anyway."

The restaurant was filled with the Elko business lunch crowd and travelers. At one round table, a family of six sat. A baby in a high chair threw a spoon to the floor. His mother picked it up, put it on the tray, and the baby threw it down again. Two other children fidgeted and looked around while an old lady with white hair talked with her mouth full of food, and gestured with her fork.

It was difficult for Sam not to stare at the beer sign above Kathy's head.

"I'll buy," he said.

"I wouldn't mind a hamburger," Katy said, searching the lists of Italian dishes and possible combinations. Items had been crossed out with a messy ballpoint pen, prices raggedly changed, upwards. "Can you find just a plain hamburger?"

Sam smiled at her as he reached for a glass of water.

"Listen, Kate, it's my birthday. We'll have a little celebration here. You can have a small steak and a plate of John's famous spaghetti, hear?" He cleared his throat. "You kids don't eat right, and then you get sick and wonder . . ." He stopped abruptly and looked away.

"Happy Birthday," she said.

"Thanks."

Grinning Johnny Leone poured the wine. He winked at Sam.

"Here's to your birthday," Katy said, raising her glass.

"Well, well, well, you old dog," Johnny said. He reached to the next table for one of the overturned water glasses and poured some Chianti into the bottom.

"Here's to you, Sam," he laughed. "Many happy returns of the day." He turned to Katy. "And to a pretty young girl."

"That's enough, John," Sam said protectively.

Johnny Leone shrugged, his round little red lip pouting underneath the mustache. "Whatever you say. . . ." He looked at Katy. "What'll you have, miss?"

Sam sighed. "She'll have this steak here, and I'll . . ." Sam kept his eyes to the menu, then to Johnny. He glanced at other people, avoiding Katy. But once, their eyes met. Katy was, after all, staring at him. And he did not blink because he knew it would be cowardly to look away. Then he poured more wine into his glass and fixed his gaze at a point across the room.

He was not going to apologize for Johnny's teasing.

A plump waitress with a very short skirt brought the food and said, "You wave, you need anything."

Katy drew her knife through the steak and Sam saw red juice spill onto the plate. She paused, put her knife and fork down and looked away. She reached for her water, took a drink, a deep breath, and picked up the utensils once again.

Sam ate quickly. His knife scraped the steak bone, making an unpleasant noise. While Katy struggled with her spaghetti, he twisted and twirled his onto his fork like a master.

"Good, huh? What did I tell you?" He smiled with his mouth, but his eyes wavered. The anxiety he thought he had conquered was returning.

Sam could hear bits of conversation though the words were muffled against the sound of dishes, the rhythmic clinking, whirring, dinging of the few slot machines lined up by the door. The lights in the room were bright spots of color, clear and steady.

"Everybody who gets their hair done at Shirley's place comes out looking the same. Makes me damned mad," said a blond woman at the table next to them.

A heavyset man with three other men laughed, then saluted with a glass of beer. "As long as Joe Rogatah is president of the Chamber of Commerce, we aren't going to get no major push for a little league park."

The businessman's lunch. There was no background music.

"You wait right here," Sam said to Katy. "I'm going back to check John's supplies." He wiped his mouth with the napkin and tossed it by the side of his plate. "Get the girlie to give you some ice cream, if you want."

"Okay," she said.

He left. She did not order ice cream. She sipped her wine

and studied the residents of Elko and the patrons of Johnny Leone's Italian restaurant.

"That's my nephew, George, in there," Johnny said as he walked with Sam toward the storeroom. "Rosa, she's yelled at him ever since she come back from the hospital."

Rosa had varicose veins that formed blue knots on her calves.

"He did all right cooking, but she rides his ass all day. Pretty soon, he'll quit and the next time Rosa's legs go out, there I'll be." Johnny chewed at his lip, tasting the short black hairs of his mustache. "Who's the girl?" Johnny asked.

"A girl who lives near us in California," Sam said. He turned his back to Johnny and began to count the boxes of concentrate left on the shelves. "I'm giving her a ride home to her family."

Through the kitchen door, Sam could hear Rosa yelling in Italian at the young man. Sam could see him chopping peppers with short strokes of a steel cleaver. He saw red spots of anger on George's cheeks, and Sam wished Rosa would shut up. The blade thudded against the wood, mincing the peppers. Johnny stepped into the kitchen and in more Italian ordered Rosa to stop shouting at the young man. Still George chopped, placing round white onions in front of him, bringing the knife down with precise lethal strokes.

Rosa, Sam thought, had a wicked mouth, a perpetually scolding look. Having completed the order, Sam stepped into the kitchen.

A large man at the grill turned away from the sizzling spit of the meat to shrug and laugh and raise his spatula to Sam in salute to the madness in the kitchen.

"And you," Rosa said, turning to Sam. "Out there with

a girl young enough to be your daughter."

Above the penetrating thudding of the knife in George's hand, Johnny cursed her again in Italian.

"Ah," she said, with a gesture of disgust at her husband, "you tell him what happened to Ignacio when he got mixed up with that teenager . . ."

Johnny, defeated, turned back to Sam. He rolled his eyes heavenward, and shrugged in apology.

"He got her you-know-what. That's what happened," Rosa continued.

It was too much. Sam advanced on her. "You ought to learn to mind your own business, Rosa," he said. "You ought to learn to keep your mouth shut."

Rosa stepped back, raising a spoon as if Sam might strike her. Except for the sound of the meat frying on the fire, the whirr of the fan, the kitchen was silent.

"Daughter," Sam hissed at her. "My daughter died two months ago. My Julianna. You hear that, Rosa?"

The young man brought the cleaver down on the board with one last thud, looked with absolute contempt at Rosa, and stormed from the kitchen.

"Oh, Sam . . ." Rosa said, lowering the spoon. "Sorry." She seemed painfully helpless.

Johnny took Sam's arm and led him back to the storeroom. The man at the grill steadily flipped the steaks and hamburgers, one side to the other, scraping the grease with long strokes into the trough.

"Hey," Johnny said quietly, "you should have told us. Sam, we didn't know."

"Oh, hell, John," Sam said. He went back into the dining room, from the light of the kitchen into the murmured darkness of the restaurant. It would be terrible to go back out into the sun. Johnny was one of his oldest customers. Why couldn't he have kept his mouth shut?

Rosa was a bitch, but that was not his business. It was John's.

When he got back to the table, Katy was gone. He leaned for a moment against his chair, then straightened, picked up the check, and turned toward the door. She must have gone to the car. She could not have overheard.

"Hey, Sam," Johnny said. "We're real sorry, both of us, real sorry."

"I'll send a shipment of concentrate out to you next week," Sam said.

"The dinner's on us, Sam. Okay?" Johnny pleaded.

"I appreciate it," Sam said, putting his wallet back into his pocket. Johnny's eyes were filled with sympathy. "Sorry I blew up," he added. "I can't seem to shake it. Christ, John," he said, feeling the tremor in his own voice, "she was only fifteen years old. A damned brain tumor."

"A sad thing," Johnny said. He patted Sam's shoulder.

"Fifteen years old," Sam repeated, shaking his head.

When he got to the station wagon, Katy was not there. He stood in the blazing Nevada sun, unable to think what to do. For a moment he was terrified that he had imagined her, that she did not exist, and then he saw her pack through the window. He did not want to go back into Johnny's and ask. Maybe she was in the ladies' room. Why hadn't he thought to check before he left? He stood with his hand on the door. Rosa with her words, Johnny with his sympathy, the sound of the cleaver hitting the board. Where could she be? He looked frantically up and down the highway. What the hell was he going to do? He could not just drive away and leave her. Abandon her.

But she had left him. Maybe she didn't care about the pack. Maybe she had gotten another ride. Maybe she was tired of listening to him talk. Why should he care?

If he could just think what to do?

The sun was killing him, the heat overpowering his reason.

The waitress. He would have to ask the waitress to check the restroom. He prayed Johnny would not ask him any more questions.

The wine had done it. Katy had run from the restaurant, pushing her way through the smoke-filled room, bumping into a man in a blue polyester cowboy suit who said, "Hey, wait a minute there, honey, where you goin' so fast?"

But she made it to the door, out into the sun, and while the gravel crunched beneath her sandals, small pebbles assaulted the bottoms of her feet, she ran around the corner of the building, around a large metallic orange van with fancy side panels of marbelized design, and mountain scenes on the screens. Between the van and an air-conditioned Buick with North Carolina plates, behind the right rear tire of the van, she lost her lunch in a pink-colored lumpy puddle, replete with sour taste and aching muscles. She leaned against the van, burning her shoulder on the hot metal.

She looked down to see one corner of her skirt stained with the vomit, sickening her again. She walked around in back of the restaurant, looking for a water faucet, the sun still beating down on her, and did not find the tap.

A young man came out the back door of Johnny's restaurant. He removed his white apron, wadded it into a ball, and threw it at the building. His eyes were bitter brown, motionless in anger as he looked at Katy. Then, without speaking, he turned and walked away.

The wet spot on her skirt brushed her ankle.

Through the parking lot and around an auto supply store was a service station. She passed the white garbage cans, the sides stained with filth, flies buzzing, loose papers scattering off into the desert. She stepped around a tumbleweed in the parking lot. Its spines were studded with hamburger papers from the Dixie Freeze and one crumpled cherry soda can.

Katy ran by the cars in back of the store, where piles of cardboard boxes waited.

A blond man held the gasoline hose in the fuel tank of a 1976 Coupe de Ville that would take at least twenty-two gallons of Supreme and watched her. Katy opened the door marked WOMEN, turned on the water faucet and scooping up and dipping her soiled skirt into the dirty sink, she scrubbed.

When she came out, the young man stood casually leaning against the Cadillac, staring at her, smiling, leering from behind sunglasses.

He said to the man seated behind the steering wheel, "That'll be twelve eighty-nine, sir," and then he turned as Katy walked by and whistled.

"Silly," she murmured and turned back toward Johnny's.

The service station attendant looked like Kurt Edwards. Kurt had told her she was pretty, too, and look what he had done. All those breathless moments. *Katy, you're the prettiest girl I've ever seen.* She'd been so certain he loved her. She wanted to turn and shake her fist at the service station attendant, but instead she walked, spreading out her skirt to dry in the sun.

Then she saw Sam. He was standing by the station wagon, and he looked like he was going to leave. She started to run.

"Wait," she called, her feet slipping in the gravel. "Mr. Batinovich." She waved her hand. She did not notice, as she ran, the motorcyclists with their trailers passing by on the street.

"Please wait," she called.

Sam turned and watched her run toward him, and before he could check himself, he was glad. "I'll wait," he said, though he knew she could not hear.

"I wasn't going to leave you," he said as he opened the door for her.

She was breathless, her hand at her throat. She could not speak.

Sam was so confused by his reaction to seeing Katy that he was nearly out of town before he remembered. He always got gas in Elko. He had driven by his regular filling station without even noticing.

"Dammit," he said. "Sorry. I just almost forgot to fill up."

"Oh," Katy said. She still panted, gasping for air from the running. "I'm sorry," she murmured. "I just wanted to look around. I thought I'd be back before you finished."

Sam resisted the impulse to lecture her and turned into the Texaco station. "The desert's no place to run out of gas," he said instead. "Of course, it's not so bad now. We used to carry water bags, did you know that?" He did not know why it mattered. "Cars used to boil easier than they do now."

He turned off the ignition. Katy still breathed heavily, her hand on her breast.

"Are you okay?" he asked.

She nodded. Perspiration shone on her forehead and on her shoulders.

"I wasn't going to leave you," he repeated.

Sam turned to the attendant who had appeared at the window and said, "Fill her with ethyl, please, and give the oil a look-see, will you?"

"Sure thing," the man said. His arms were greasy, and his clothes black marked. He wiped his hands on a dirty towel. In red letters, embroidered on the pocket of his green shirt, was his name. Alf.

"What's a water bag?" Katy asked. She kept tugging at her skirt, at her waist. She seemed uncomfortable.

"Like a kind of canvas-burlap canteen. Used to carry it for drinking and in case the car boiled over."

The attendant opened the hood.

"You're a quart low," the man said, holding the dip stick for Sam to see. Even the attendant's bushy blond eyebrows had traces of grease.

"Ten–fortyW. . ." Sam said.

The smell of gasoline and oil was pervasive. Sam wondered how mechanics stood it.

A car pulled in on the other side of the pump. The man got out and stood by his door, waiting for service. He wore a white short-sleeved shirt and a necktie. He drove the frill-free car furnished by a company. Beige, no chrome. Blackwall tires.

Sam laughed. Pencimil always let him pick his own car, and Sam loved the new wagon. These big companies. The man looked annoyed. Impatient. He drummed his fingers on the roof of his car.

Alf came out of the garage with a can of oil, spout inserted. The dirty rag hung from his waist.

"Be with you in a minute," Alf said to the man. He disappeared under the hood.

"Mr. Ferguson?" the man in the necktie asked.

"Yes, sir," Alf answered.

"I'm Arthur Bowman. I'm the Texaco station inspector

for this region. I'll be looking around." He took a hand-kerchief from his back pocket and wiped his nose.

Alf slammed the hood.

"Terrific," he said. "What a day." He shook his head. "Two of my men are off sick and the other one's wife is having a baby. I'm here all alone."

"I'll park over there," Arthur Bowman said.

A camper from Nebraska pulled into the station.

"Things sure pile up," Sam said to Alf as he finished filling the tank.

Three men on motorcycles zoomed into the station drowning out Alf's response.

Arthur Bowman got out of his car with a clipboard in hand. He walked directly to the garage, assumed a stance, and began marking on the paper attached to the board.

"Nine seventy-seven," Alf said, and Sam handed him a credit card.

The camper pulled out of the station. The motor-cyclists were taking care of themselves. Sam saw Alf talking on the telephone in the station.

"Hey, man, we're in a hurry," the shortest cyclist shouted.

"They aren't Hell's Angels," Katy said.

"They must be the three stooges then," Sam muttered.

"My brother wants a motorcycle."

"Great. The one who already cracked up the car? Great. Your old man can probably get one of his doctor buddies to patch the kid up for nothing when he breaks his head."

"We have to pay," Katy sighed, "just like everyone else."

"Somehow I doubt that."

"Well, we do."

"You better have plenty of insurance then—or at least your father should. Medical bills can wipe a person out."

They had been lucky, Sam thought, to have insurance. Who would have thought a fourteen-year-old girl, his girl, could get so sick?

Alf came to the window with the credit card clipboard. Arthur Bowman was still checking boxes in the garage.

"Martinez's wife just had a ten-pound baby boy," Alf said. "How about that."

A Winnebago motor home with Utah plates pulled into the station.

"These boobs," said the motorcyclist with the leather vest and bare chest. "Like a fuckin' turtle, carrying his fuckin' house."

The man in the motor home rolled up his window.

"There," said Sam as he finished signing. "Good luck."

"What a day," Alf sighed. "But Martinez, he's coming right over to work."

The shortest biker waved at Katy, and she waved back.

"Those are no types for you to fool around with," Sam said as he drove out of the station.

"I don't know how they can be any worse than these clean-cut college boys," Katy said and closed her eyes.

"Well, you might be surprised," Sam warned. What did she mean by that, he wondered. Kids, naive. Dumb. They would walk up to Jack the Ripper and invite him to lunch. He'd worried about Julianna, about the boys she knew. What if one hurt her? Molested her. What would he do? Wasn't that the damned irony of the whole thing. He was going to protect her, yes sir. Screen those boys that came to call. No one was going to hurt his girl.

"My mother wrote a short story once," Katy said, "about a housewife who wanted to be a Hell's Angel."

That was a new one, Sam thought. He would recommend that to Thelma. The house had filled, in the last few months, with new hobbies, new things to keep Thelma's mind off the inevitable. Friends took her to meetings, to lectures. She had made new curtains for the kitchen and the bedroom, and he hadn't liked them as well as the old ones.

The three motorcyclists roared around them, one at a time. Katy sat up and opened her eyes at the sound. Then the bikers formed a line and rode three abreast. Like performers who hear a count that is lost to the audience, in unison, each raised a black-gloved hand in a power salute to Sam and Katy.

Sam gripped the steering wheel and refused to blink.

Katy said, "Wow."

The motorcyclists fell out of formation and sped away. Soon they were three tiny dots on the road that led west.

"What town is next?" Katy asked.

"Carlin," Sam said. "They have an ice-packing plant there. Used to fill up the refrigerated train cars. Carlin is high and damned cold in the winter."

Katy leaned back against the seat. Her eyes were closed.

"Good place for ice," he went on. He had driven this road so many times. "Next is Battle Mountain. Lots of turquoise there. I bought my wife a ring once. A little round stone set in the middle of a silver flower." Did Thelma still wear it? He could not remember. "The man who sold it to me was one of the real town characters, could give you the history of everything. The massacre in 1861. 'Settlers chased down and killed them damned Indians,' he would say." Sam rubbed his chin. "Sometimes the guy talked just like he had been there himself, right there at Gravelly Ford. And he knew everything about turquoise; what was good and what was common. Funny old guy, I suppose he's dead now. He hated the Indians, talked like they were about to attack any time."

Sam looked at the mountains. Not so much as a stick

of a building to be seen. He could understand, for the
first time, how the man felt. It was true. The land looked
the same way now as it would have then. He could imagine an Indian warrior on a horse overlooking the highway. Like an Indian in a western painting. Wouldn't be
so strange to see one after all. Maybe, back in the hills,
back where the narrow dirt roads disappeared into noth-
ingness, a lost tribe . . .

He laughed.

Indians rode motorcycles now.

But it wouldn't seem strange at all to see a brave on a
horse on the timeless hills. Nevada was out of phase with
the cities, with the twentieth century. An Indian on a
horse.

"I always wanted to stay around longer and listen to
the old man. Probably could have learned more history
from him than from any book."

Katy shifted in the seat, and Sam turned to look at her.
Her eyes were closed, then suddenly open, as if she could
feel him looking at her.

"What did you say?" she asked.

"You just sleep," Sam said softly. "Just go back to
sleep."

Katy was asleep. The new green tile tunnels before Carlin, she missed. Carlin, itself, she slept through and Sam was left alone with his thoughts. He tapped his fingers lightly on the steering wheel. He was jittery, jumpy. He could not forget the pained look on Johnny Leone's face.

He cleared his throat. Once, then again. A sound to break the pattern. His nose tingled and a faint sickening smell alarmed him.

Something wrong. He looked at Katy. The air conditioner whirred; the pink and blue streamers danced. The smell came and went again, eluding identification. To his dismay, he noticed he was gripping the steering wheel too tightly. White circles at the knuckles. One minute he felt fine. Relaxed, happy. The next, like his heart was beating too fast. As if he were afraid. He released, tightened, tried to find the balance and could not. The smell rushed by him again and escaped. He shifted uncomfortably in his seat and stared ahead at the road without actually seeing.

Suddenly he wished he was alone. He considered he might talk to himself. It was a frightening impulse. Craziness. It was the wine. His nerves. His confusion when he could not find Katy. He could not afford to depend upon someone, anyone that way. Not even Thelma.

The broken white lines in the center of the highway
sped by him like so many evenly spaced dashes into the
heart. Transfixed, he saw them flying at him. Horrified,
he could think of no good reason, right at that moment, to
be alive. He imagined cutting those lines with a quick
right angle of the steering wheel, whipping the car per-
pendicular to the oncoming dashes, banking it into a skid
and then rolling side over side, off into the sagebrush.
Rolling with the tumbleweeds, capturing broken glass and
crushed aluminum cans and pieces of brush and cedar.
Winding, rolling along with the screams and the broken
glass and the crushing metal, compressing, but ending, and
escaping the steadiness of those oncoming perfectly spaced
white pieces of line that represented the rest of the days
of his life.

He stopped the thought. He tried to laugh at the melo-
drama of it all. He had to be careful. He did not want to
be so taken with the fantasy that he accidentally became
part of it. He guessed he did not want to die like Julianna
had, a day at a time, weakening eyes, fingers that could
barely hold onto his own. Not like that.

Sam rubbed his jaw with his thumb. He could see it so
clearly when he tried. The rolling white station wagon,
the screams. He had rammed a wood-carving gouge into
the palm of his hand once, and he imagined that the first
bone-crushing puncture would be a pain like that, only
one thousand times worse.

Why couldn't he drop it? Morbid, he thought, simple
morbid preoccupation.

The Batinoviches die on their birthdays, it would say
in a record book somewhere. Sam swallowed. Something
about the sentence appealed to him. Would shake some
people off their pins. He thought he must be losing his
mind.

Vomit. The smell was one of sickness. Vomit. Something was the matter with the young girl who sat next to him, her arms thin and colorless. Sick. She moved. He could tell she was not asleep. He could hear her having difficulty swallowing, taking short sharp breaths.

"Listen," he said, "you sick to your stomach?"

Katy did not open her eyes.

"You hear me? I asked if you are sick or something?"

With the static motion of a blind person, feeling through perpetual darkness, Katy raised her hands in front of her.

"I, yes, sick. Stop the car. Please." One of the rigid hands moved to her mouth. She sat up straight. Her eyes widened, and she seemed to have difficulty seeing.

"Please . . ."

The Palisade turnoff was ahead. Sam pressed on the brake and eased off and down away from the highway. A calmness straightened his arms and his thoughts. He was careful not to slam the brakes and thrust Katy forward. He turned onto the road to Mary's Creek. It pointed north toward the solitary mountains and Katy, still blindly keeping her sickness contained with a hand, reached for the door handle, struggled, found it, and as soon as Sam stopped, she opened the door and leaned out.

Sam set the brake, got out of the car, and hurried to Katy's side. Her head hung down, her hair streaming so that he could not see her face. Through gasping sobs came the angry wrenching of her stomach, small streams of spittle and what tiny morsels remained from her lunch.

"Oh," she murmured through tears. "Sorry."

Sam wanted to take her hair and pull it away from her face. He needed to do something to help her. Or make her stop. Useless. Like before. Standing by helplessly while tubes and bottles were inserted into Julianna's poor body. The illusive veins. Bruises. He had wanted to pick her up from that hospital bed and carry her away, but she was trapped, confined by the lifegiving liquids, clear and eventually useless. And here Katy was, held by her hair that covered her face and muffled her words. Sam could not see any way to help her out of the car unless she could stop the convulsive retching long enough to stand.

"Come on," he whispered. "See if you can get out of the car. We can walk."

What remained of the asphalt road north was broken and chunky. Only the part nearest the turnoff had been paved and where a dirt road had gone somewhere, sometime, sagebrush grew, and the road no longer existed. Sam did not have time to wonder, as he usually did, what was at the end of that road, or who lived at Mary's Creek.

"Come on," he urged. "You'll feel better if we walk a little."

She pushed her hair back from her wet face. Her eyes lowered, her body shaking, she slid out of the car, carefully sidestepping the puddle of vomit. She was unsteady on her feet. The gravel slipped beneath her.

Sam took her hands, then put his arm around her waist. He had walked like this before, some woman who had too much to drink. When was that? Who was she?

Katy leaned against him, tears streaming from her face. Quiet crying now. Hurt crying. Not spoiled or willful cries. He could always tell the difference with Julianna. He had been home one day when Julianna came in from her first grade class in tears. "Johnny Martin said I had ugly toes." Sam had taken her in his arms and laughed until she laughed with him. Thelma never could tell the difference the way he could. If Julianna cried, she held her, soothed her, held her as tightly as she could. So when Julianna cried at last, "My head is bursting with this pain. Am I going to die soon?" Thelma couldn't hold her any tighter, could not comfort her enough. Sam had sat down on the bed and cried with her.

"Isn't your father a doctor?" he asked Katy, then the absurdity of the question embarrassed him.

He put his arm around her and she covered her face with her hands. Together they walked away from the station wagon, down the road that led nowhere.

"No . . ." Katy moaned. "Stop."

They turned toward the side of the road. She bent over and the racking heaves began again, dry now. She choked tiny bubbles of saliva onto the parched, cracked desert earth. Sam stood behind her, holding her around her middle. She seemed too weak to stand. He could feel the terrible contracting of her stomach. He wanted to rest his cheek against the back of her neck and hold her, make her feel better. The tears were hot on her face and she gagged. He wanted to cry; he wanted to moan with her. He could feel every muscle of her body held tight against him. He curved over her to protect and hold her, his face close now, into her hair.

"Oh God," she cried. "I wish I was dead." Another gasping contraction from her abdomen.

Again the vision of the station wagon rolling over, slowly now, stop motion, crashing almost delicately, the glass flying in slight silver threads, clearly enough to seem like strings of tinsel, sprinkles of glitter in the sun.

Her buttocks shook against him, stimulating him and angering him. He held her tighter, whispering, "It's okay, now, don't worry, you'll be okay."

"Need any help here?" a man asked.

Sam blinked. He turned and saw a man in green walking shorts and a white shirt. The sun was too bright. He could not think.

"We wondered if you needed some help?" the man repeated. "We saw you from the road."

Sam, still holding Katy around the waist, looked past the man. He squinted at the blue sedan. What was wrong?

"She's okay," he stammered.

The man did not move.

"She's all right now," Sam said. He wanted to yell at the man to go away. He was embarrassing Katy. "I tell you, she'll be okay." People did not like others to see them when they were sick. Everyone knew that. *I don't want them to see me,* Julianna had said, touching a thin hand to her few remaining strands of hair.

Katy sniffed, turned, and clung to Sam.

"Are you all right, miss?"

"Yes," she choked. "Really."

The man now seemed ominous to Sam. Why the hell didn't he get back in his car? Sam could handle the situation. Dammit, he could handle it.

Without expression, the man said, "I've got some pills here, for motion sickness." He stepped forward, his hand outstretched with the packet.

The voice, familiar. The vision. Sam blinked. He looked at the sedan and a meeting of sun and mirror blinded him, leaving a dark star before his eyes. The man's shirt was blazing white. Like a doctor's hospital coat.

Sam took the pills, still holding onto Katy.

"Thank you," he muttered, and the man stepped back. "I can take care of her now. Thank you."

A little girl in a yellow sunsuit leaned from the car window and called, "Daddy, Daddy."

Katy whispered, "I'm all right now, really . . ."

Sam wanted to pick her up and carry her away. Hold her like a baby. Don't drop a baby. Soft furry head. Soft spot. Feel the brain. Gently, firmly. Don't let her go. Soft spot decaying. He would pick her up and wade through the sea with her, holding her safe.

"Miss, would you rather ride with us?"

A doctor, a priest, a judge. Hopeless, a month, maybe two. Pray for her, pray. You didn't do enough. Sentence. You shouldn't have waited. Five years—ten to life.

"Get out of here," Sam shouted.

Katy started to cry. Sam tried to be gentle, but his hands were stiff.

"Sssh, shh," he tried to whisper, but his words were too loud.

"Miss?"

Katy shook her head. "No. He's taking me home. Thank you . . . please."

The man took another step backward on the road. He was unbending in the sun. His eyes did not leave Sam's face.

Damned staring bastard. Sam felt Katy's hair next to his face, and she seemed to be getting smaller. Her cries were whimpers now, breath-catching like a little girl's. He watched the man retreat while fat white clouds gathered behind him in the hot blue sky. Round thick clouds rising up from the horizon. The man stood flat against them.

"We only offer Christian help," the man said in the same even tone.

"Daddy, Daddy, come on."

Sam had difficulty keeping the man in focus. His eyes trembled, his face was tight. Katy, poor sick girl, leaning against him, shaking. His hands were too large to be kind, his heart too raw to comfort her enough.

"I can take care of my daughter," Sam shouted while the bright splinters of light pierced his skull. "I can take care of my daughter."

They sat in the station wagon. Sam did not know how much time had elapsed. Daughter. Had he shouted to the man? Daughter. Or had he merely imagined it. Were his hands shaking enough for her to see? He tried to laugh.

"Damned do-gooders," he muttered.

He looked over his shoulder to see if the road was clear to enter the highway. He did not want to see Katy's face. *Daughter.* He could not escape the feeling that he had been in the place before. Helpless. Someone accusing, demanding, suggesting. Doctors. But this time, by God, he had said something. Taken action. Gravel whipped the underside of the wagon as he pushed the accelerator, then the wheels caught the pavement and they moved up onto the highway. Crazy, he almost said aloud. Crazy thoughts. Katy wasn't his problem. He tried to convince himself that she had nothing to do with the clouded memories that pressed him on his birthday. Of course. The years passing, he shouldn't be mad with her. *With her.* Words his mother used. Old country. *At her.* He corrected the dialogue of his thought.

"Feeling okay now?"

"Yes."

"You should have told me you were carsick. We could have gotten some Dramamine at Johnny's."

"It doesn't work once you're sick," she said.

"I guess you doctors' daughters know things like that."

"He didn't tell me that; I just know."

He was sorry that he had pushed at her. She seemed about to cry.

"You act like because my father's a doctor, I don't get sick, that things don't happen to me, and that's not true." Her voice clearly trembled.

"I'm sorry," Sam said. "I didn't mean . . ."

"My father thinks I can take care of myself, anyway. That's what they all think. Everyone except for you."

He was astonished at the tone of her voice. All he had tried to do was help.

"Well, I don't see how you're doing such a great job of taking care of yourself. Hitchhiking home like a bum."

"You don't have to help me anymore."

He sighed. "Now look, Katy. I don't mind helping you. I'm sorry you're sick. I just wouldn't let my own daughter . . ."

"You probably wouldn't let her do anything."

A barely perceptible pulse began in Sam's head. *I let her die.* He sniffed. He tried to swallow the rising tightness in his throat.

"And why did you say I was your daughter?"

"Daughter?" Did the words sound choked? Wrung from hell knows where in his soul? *Daughter.* He did not want to tell her about Julianna. He could not endure more questions. This girl was not his daughter.

"Why did you do that?" she asked again.

He shifted in the seat. "Listen, young lady, that man seemed to have peculiar ideas about what was going on."

Yes, that was right.

"Now you might not care what people think of you, but I'm a businessman and I can't afford that kind of dirty-minded thinking going on about me."

Gossip. The kind Rosa loved. He wasn't going to put up with it. All he wanted to do was stop the man. And he had.

"I can't afford to have people think I'm taking advantage of some young girl. You see?"

"I just don't think you owed him any explanation."

"Well, we working men stick with convention, you might say." He could be sarcastic, too. This girl was not his daughter. She was not a child; she was a young woman he did not know. He felt sorry for her because she was sick. That was all of it.

Two Neptune moving vans traveling together, identical

yellow trucks with red letters, passed them going east.

"That was embarrassing," Katy said. "I'm sorry."

"You always get carsick like that?" Sam asked.

Katy looked out the window at the empty landscape. The hills and mountains were barren, one-toned. There was no one out there. Like a poisoned area.

"Not usually. Maybe I ate something that didn't agree with me."

Sam laughed. "Well, John's spaghetti can pack a wallop." He needed to ease up. They passed another camper on the road, and a little boy waved at them. *Have you hugged your kid today?* the bumper sticker asked.

"A wallop, like a fista in the stomacho." Italiano. Like a joke. Last year, on one of his trips through, Cora had told him a great joke. A classic. He wondered if Katy knew any jokes. Julianna with her book of elephant jokes. Riddles. He could not remember them. A long time ago. *Katy was not his daughter.*

"You got other brothers and sisters," Sam asked, "besides the one who wrecked the car?"

"Another one in the seventh grade," Katy said. "He's a genius on the computer."

"You sure have an odd family," Sam added. "A doctor, a mother who writes stories, a grandmother who wants to ride a motorcycle."

"I'm the only one who doesn't know what I want to do," Katy said.

She was huddled in the corner, her denim jacket pulled around her shoulders.

"You going to college in the fall?"

"I don't think so."

"Too cold in here for you?" he asked. "We can turn the freezer down some if you want."

"I'm okay," she whispered.

"You should go. You'll be sorry if you don't. Your parents will be disappointed."

"They won't care."

He thought she might be going to cry. She acted like her parents didn't love her. That couldn't be true. Parents always loved their children.

"Of course they care."

"You don't know them. They just want me to be a *fulfilled individual*."

"So what's wrong with that? So your parents want you to be happy. Is that such a crime?"

"You don't understand."

"I understand more than you think." Spoiled, Sam thought. Pure and simple. His Julianna knew they loved her. She was never a minute of trouble. Never. He wanted to shout at Katy, you're so damned lucky to be alive.

"My mother and father are separate distinct individuals," Katy said, "and they see us—my brothers and me —in the same way. It's just that sometimes, they don't seem . . ."

"Sounds to me as if you've had everything you ever wanted or needed, and probably then some."

They rode in silence then. Katy pushed the cuticles of her fingers down with her thumb nail. Sam kept his eyes on the road, his mouth set in a line.

Finally he sighed. "Listen," he said. "You want to hear a joke?"

"I guess," Katy answered.

"I know this woman. Cora. She owns the cafe at the junction. She knows the best damned jokes. Serves them up with breakfast."

"What kind of jokes does she tell?" Katy asked.

"Truck driver jokes, dirty jokes."

"I don't know any jokes like that," she said.

"Well, you probably don't hang around with truck drivers."

Sam laughed.

"What kind of jokes do you know?" he asked.

"I guess I don't know any at all," Katy said. "Aren't most of those jokes macho things, anti-feminist?"

"Forget it."

Katy scowled at him.

"I wish to hell I had a cigarette," Sam said.

"I didn't mean you were a male chauvinist or anything, it's just that most jokes . . ."

"You don't need to hear this one."

She rolled her eyes at the roof of the car and sighed. "I didn't mean to make you angry again."

Sam spoke, his mouth tense, his eyes on the road. "Listen, I was trying to cheer you up. My mistake. You probably wouldn't get it anyhow."

Now it was important to tell the joke. He wanted to laugh himself. He wanted to forget the look on Johnny's face, Cora, lonely in the door of the cafe. He wanted to forget Julianna's last day. *See the birthday cake, baby. It's pink, your favorite color.* They had talked to her as if she were a two year old, and she was a dying fifteen. *Oh, baby, see the cake. See the pretty pink roses. Mama will cut you a rose. Happy Birthday to you, happy birthday to you.*

"It's just that—well, sex jokes tend to put women down."

"Well, this joke puts down men, and Italians, and wrestlers. There isn't a woman in the whole joke," Sam said. "Besides, like I told you, a woman told it to me."

Katy looked out at the passing desert, miles of flat high brush, twisted angry trees scratching at the sky, clumps of blue cedar pinned to their arms. Prairie dogs popped up from the holes along the highway and sat motionless, paws in prayerful pose. Quick. Rabbits occasionally white-tailed under the fences, up over the rise alongside the road. Sometimes they ran directly into cars, and the fur-splotched remains were splattered on the highway, and the magpies and black birds picked at the reddened mess. Katy saw the delicate ears of a long-dead rabbit blowing transparently like flower petals growing from the pavement.

A lone black crow sat on a rock and waited for them to pass.

Then she said, "Actually, I'd like to hear the joke. I guess most of my friends think they're too smart to tell a funny joke."

Sam relaxed. "Well, you better laugh," he warned. "It's a long joke."

He tried to remember Cora's gestures. It was like erasing the look of pity in her eyes. He tried to recall how his Uncle Tony exaggerated his Italian accent so the joke would be as funny as possible.

"Well," he began, "There was thisa Italian wrestler named Giuseppe and he wanted to be the champion of the worlda."

Sam loved the joke. The accent sounded pretty good, he thought, as he explained how Giuseppe's manager went about setting up three matches for the wrestler. "If you beata the Spaniard, the Englishaman, and the Germana, you bea the champion."

Sam's face twitched with the concentration and the anticipation. Katy sat with her hands folded, her mouth tightly shut.

"Giuseppe, he hada no trouble with the Englishman or the Spanish guy, so the manager, he sets up the match with the German.

" 'Now, Guiseppe,' the manager say, 'this German, he the toughest of 'em alla. He gotta this pretzel hold. No mattera what happens, don't let him getta you into the pretzela holda.' Giuseppe, he nodda and the match begins. The manager, he stands and yells at Giuseppe, 'Dona let him getta ya into the pretzela holda.'

"So these two big guys are wrestling away and the manager can see that the German is getting Giuseppe into a pretzel hold. He's wrapping his legs and arms around Giuseppe's neck, and they're getting all twisted up. Then he can see it is too late. Giuseppe is finally caught in the pretzela holda."

Sam stopped to snicker.

"The manager, he give up, throws down the towel and starts to leave. He's just about to the door when he hears a big cheer, and he turns around expecting to see Giuseppe lying on the mat, and there was his man; they were holding his arm in the air. Giuseppe had won the matcha."

Katy squirmed in the seat, a static smile on her face.

"And the manager, he ran back to the ring and threw his arms around Giuseppe and he said, 'What happena, what happena?' And Giuseppe, who was all out of breath said, 'We wasa all tangled up. My arms around his heada, my legs around his necka, his face I couldna see and all of a sudden, I seea this big pair a ballsa right above me. They're a-swinging backa and a fortha, backa and fortha, so I reach up and take a big bite-a.' "

Suddenly, Sam wished he had used the word *testicles,* but it was too late.

Katy managed a nervous giggle.

" 'What happena then?' the manager yells.

" 'Wella,' Giuseppe said, 'there's no holda thata you cannota breaka, when you bite-a your own ballsa!' "

Sam started to laugh. He slapped the steering wheel with his hand. It was his favorite joke. He shook his head in delight.

Katy was astonished.

"There is no holda thata you cannota breaka when you bite-a your own ballsa." He threw back his head. He did not seem to notice that Katy was not laughing.

"Listen," Sam said, clearing his throat but still smiling. "Don't go home and tell that to your father. He wouldn't appreciate me telling his daughter a joke like that."

He would never have told his own daughter, his Juli. But didn't that make it clear? He knew who was what, and who was where.

"I think my father had an affair with his nurse once," Katy said.

"Well, don't tell it anyway," Sam commanded. Why did Katy tell him that? Doctors. "That Cora has hundreds of jokes." He wondered why he couldn't remember any other ones.

They rode in silence through Battle Mountain, by the turquoise shops and the train station. Katy looked out the window at the few people on the street in the sun, and Sam watched the speed limit and the traffic light.

"There's where I got the ring I told you about," he said, pointing to one of the shops. "It's a shame about the crack in the stone."

The big block white letters on the mountain ahead always amused Sam. BM. Battle Mountain wasn't much of a place in his opinion.

"By the way," Katy asked as they resumed normal speed. "I've been meaning to ask. Do you have a daughter?"

Ahead, a heavyset woman in a fluorescent orange vest turned the circular sign she held from SLOW to STOP.

"No, I don't have a daughter. Notice how they got mostly lady flagmen nowadays? Christ, that would be a hell of a job."

"They must make plenty of money," Katy said. "As much as a man."

Sam tightened his hand on the steering wheel. "Money doesn't mean much to someone who's been run down by one of those dirt haulers. It's a damned dangerous job."

"Her family could probably sue someone." Katy smiled. "You sure talk about death a lot."

Sam felt the blood pound in his temple. Death. He stared at the woman who held the sign in front of the right fender and tried to calm down.

The woman wore Levi's that were too tight around the middle, and a yellow blouse. Except for the breasts and the short pony tail at the back of her neck, she would have been mistaken for a man. The hardhat was low over her face, and the dark glasses contributed to the disguise. A dirt hauler roared across the road in front of them, spilling enough dirt to lay the base for dusty tire tracks.

"Come on," Sam muttered. The woman still held the

sign. He rolled down the window, but before he could get his question to her, the woman held up three fingers and pointed to the left. Evenly spaced, he could see three more trucks coming toward the highway.

He thought about a crow sitting on a fence post. Right, he wanted to say, I do talk about death a lot. It's sitting on me just like the crow sits on the fence. Black. Stinking. Because he was afraid, he said in a trembling voice, "This road is always torn up somewhere. Makes you wonder."

Katy turned to look at the steadily increasing line behind them. Three back was the camper with the man in the cowboy hat. Katy could see the woman with him sitting calmly filing her fingernails, holding them up to inspect them.

"It's too bad," she said, as if he hadn't spoken, "that you can sue people for some things and not for others." She wondered if she could sue Kurt Edwards. If they could find him. That would be wonderful. He would probably deny ever knowing her. Theoflora and Melvin and Meliss were all going to insist she have an abortion. Her mother would write a poem about it. "My Daughter's Abortion." She would read it to her women's group. Wednesday evening. Camembert and Wheat Thin crackers; Zinfandel and English tea. The poem would be composed of flowers and odd hospital terms. Violets and catheters. Baby's breath and suction machines. Awful. She would not agree to it.

"Your father ever been sued for malpractice?"

Katy laughed a little, the contrast startling in the dust-filled air. "Not yet," she said. "Not yet."

"Well, he's been lucky then, in my opinion."

Another truck barreled across, kicking up the just settled dirt, bouncing and banging in the desert silence.

"They sure drive fast," Katy said, wanting to change

the subject. *Lucky*. Sam didn't know anything about her father—why would he make such a nasty remark?

"They've only got three speeds," Sam muttered. "Stopped, fast, and faster. Imagine what the kidneys are like after driving one of those for a couple of years."

Sam turned and looked back at the caravan and saw a young man in white pants and shirt walking along the shoulder of the highway.

"My hell," he said, "that's Johnny's nephew."

The young man carried a blue bag, and his dark hair fell just over his ears, rough cut as if he had angrily done it himself. He pulled at one side of his beard.

Katy turned to look. "Where?" she asked.

"The kid walking along. George. That's his name."

Katy saw the top of a young man's head as he bent to talk with someone in a car two back of them.

"I saw him, too," Katy said, excitedly. "He came out of the back door of Mr. Leone's restaurant. I'm sure it's him. He threw his apron at the building."

"Oh, that Rosa," Sam scowled. "She was giving him hell. Poor kid. Don't blame him for walking out."

The earth moved as another truck rumbled by in front of them.

George was knocking on the side window of the car in back of them. The woman did not roll down the window. She looked at him and shook her head.

Sam waved out the window at him. George stared for a minute, as if he did not understand. Then he ran around to Sam's window.

"Mr. Batinovich, could I get a ride with you?" he pleaded. "Just into Winnemucca."

The last truck thundered by in front of them, and the woman in the vest turned her sign from STOP to SLOW and waved Sam on.

Sam could not think. Rosa screaming in Italian. The steady slamming of the cleaver against the block. Katy leaned over to see, touching Sam's arm as she did so.

"Please, Mr. Batinovich, only to Winnemucca. I can get another job there." The young man begged.

The car in back of Sam honked. From down the line came the distinctive blast of a diesel truck.

"Get around there," Sam yelled, "get around to the other side. Kate, open the damned door for him."

George ran in front of the car and Sam almost stepped on the gas. He could have killed him. More horns. The woman with the sign started toward him.

Katy opened the door, and Sam pressed the gas pedal to the floor before the boy was seated. The tires squealed, then grabbed, and Katy was pushed against Sam, the young man and his pack wedged in the front seat.

"Hi. Just a minute. Let's get the pack over the seat," Katy said.

Sam had the impression he had nearly run down the flagwoman, too, and in his mind was the thought that perhaps she deserved it. Fat stinking woman out in the dirt of the man's world. Dyke. Most likely, a dyke. He was perspiring. Katy was so close to him he could smell the vomit again. The two young people struggled to get the boy's pack situated in the back. Katy was on her knees, her buttocks uncomfortably close to Sam, her back to the front of the car.

"Thanks, Mr. Batinovich," the young man said.

"Johnny know you left town?"

"Not yet."

"You should have told him," Sam stammered.

The young man opened his mouth to say something, changed his mind, and looked out the side window.

"Rosa's back," he said after a minute. "They don't need me that much."

"What are you going to do in Winnemucca?" Katy asked.

"I've got a cousin in the restaurant business there," George said.

"Soon as you get into Winnemucca, you call and tell John where you are, so he won't worry," Sam said. He sounded like a father. *Father*. Suddenly he remembered. This kid knew about Julianna. He hoped he wouldn't say anything in front of Katy. Not now. He didn't want to explain.

He felt both of them turn to look at him. He stiffened, his arms against the steering wheel, and cleared his throat. Rosa had yelled at that kid. He'd heard it himself. He didn't blame him for running out. People had more freedom these days, for better or worse. They didn't have to stick it out the way he did, running that damned farm. He'd wanted to go to college, go away somewhere. Travel. Anywhere. But his father had the stroke, and Sam stayed home and ran the farm while his father stared from his straight wooden chair in the kitchen, black dull eyes like a dead man's, one perpetual dirty look for six damned years until the bastard's black eyes closed and didn't open again. Gustave Batinovich. His father. The kids thought he was a madman. The old Yugoslavs agreed. "The Montenegrin," they said, "like his father before him, the mad Montenegrin."

And Sam's mother had danced around the man, trying to please him, setting Yugoslavian delicacies in front of his vicious stare. "You don't know," she would whisper to Sam, "all the things that man has been through."

Even with the old man dead, Sam could not think of anything good about him. Sam imagined he would pay, however, for the disrespect to his father's spirit.

But he had stayed until one of his sisters finally got a husband who liked to farm.

It was too crowded in the station wagon. Katy's thigh touched Sam's now whenever there was the slightest irregularity in the highway. Otherwise it required perfect balance. They were an hour or so from Winnemucca and the young man smelled like fried food, dust, and sweat. Sam thought he should not mind, after all George had been through, but it irritated him anyway.

Katy's shoulder, he noticed, was too close to the tight muscled bicep. And George's pants and tee shirt were so tight they could have been his skin.

"I live in Berkeley. I spent the last few months in Colorado, but I'm going home for a while," Katy said.

"Never been to Berkeley. Pretty swinging place, I hear."

"That's what people think who don't live there," Katy smiled at him.

For a while? Was he giving Katy a ride all the way, or at least part of the way, home just so she could walk out and go someplace else the next week? Couldn't anyone stay put? They were all the time leaving, leaving like Julianna had.

"I don't know," Katy said. "I thought Colorado would be different, but when I got there, most of the kids were from California."

"Even in Colorado, huh?" George said, shaking his head.

"They looked just like my old friends at home."

"You should have come to Nevada," he said. "Nobody much comes here to stay."

Why hadn't he left that farm sooner? Why hadn't he gone out the back door the way this George had done? Why hadn't he ridden off on a motorcycle? And he wouldn't have thrown any white apron at the door. He would have picked up a pitchfork and slammed it through the screen door, sticking it in the wire, tines threatening anyone who might have followed.

It was different now. Katy with her doctor father and a big house in the hills. An allowance. Time and space. Money to travel, to go to school. Probably could go to any college she wanted, *if* she wanted. He was going to give all of that to Julianna, so how could he criticize. But he wouldn't have let her go away.

"I worked in a restaurant in Vail for a while. It wasn't too bad."

"I like the cooking, but hell, old Rosa . . ."

"What do you like to cook best?"

"Well, Italian food's the thing I know."

Sam could feel them getting closer. He thought Katy moved away from him. Some kind of heat. He could feel it, and his own rose into his face. Any minute he expected to see the kid place one of his hands on Katy's knee. As if it were his own hand, he could feel the soft fabric of her skirt. He remembered holding her, the soft thin cloth, her wrenching body beneath it. He waited for the kid to start inching that way.

What the hell was wrong with him? He coughed. Protective. That's it. She reminds me. Julianna. But there Juli had been, dying in that bed, her poor little breasts shriveling with the rest of her body. One day, he had been aroused at the sight of them. He had to leave the room. He cried with self-disgust. He could not believe his own evil.

He looked at the mountains. He checked the speedometer. He turned the air conditioning up a little, flicked at a dead butterfly on the dashboard, and paid attention to the smashed bugs on the windshield. He thought about what Kristopoulis would need for his place in Winnemucca. He scratched his cheek. The glare from the sun cut a hot slash across his lap. He looked at the boy's groin, expecting to see it swollen, and he could not tell. They talked in low tones, but he could hear; he could not understand. Did they think he was asleep at the wheel?

"Yes. I liked the mountains. It's really pretty around Vail."

"Do much skiing?"

"A boy I knew was really good, and he did a fair job of teaching me, but he left . . . suddenly this summer, you might say," Katy said.

Sam cleared his throat again, and they ignored him. Damn, there was something wrong. He knew it. Any minute something was going to happen. The kid would say something about Julianna. Sam had difficulty swallowing. He could not control his thoughts though he tried staring at the highway, looking at each driver he passed. He could not get away.

Katy turned around and leaned back over the seat, reaching for something from her pack, or, Sam thought, pretending to reach. He could not see one of the kid's hands. Was he touching her breast? She could lift her skirt up, and he could be fingering her, and Sam would not be able to see because her back blocked his view.

The smell again, faint, sick. He heard her rummaging around, and she then began to settle back into the seat. She had taken the denim jacket from her pack again, and she put it around her shoulders. She was cold. The air conditioner was turned up too high. Arctic. Sam shivered.

"Sorry," he muttered. "Too cold for you, huh?" Small laugh.

"It's okay," Katy said, and rubbed the sides of her arms beneath the jacket.

Sam imagined George touching her arms, and it was

as if he touched them himself. Julianna's thin arms, almost bones against the sheets.

The station wagon warmed immediately, a testimony to the temperature outside, and Katy took off her jacket. She laid it across her lap.

George sat relaxed, his hands loosely folded in his lap, his shoulders square, his knees apart, jiggling with the motion of the station wagon. Sam could see that George's leg did touch Katy's, and he once again searched the blanket-bare desert for something to hold on to, some interesting sight to distract him. The blonde on the Johnny Carson show with her sequin shirt. Everyone was laughing. The girl, the audience. Everyone but Sam. Sex. His own daughter. No, no one knew anything about his thoughts. Thelma. In his mind she looked at him suspiciously. Damn you, Thelma, he thought. The camper passed them. The woman stared down at Sam; when he looked at her, she smiled. He checked the speedometer. Forty-five. No wonder. Holding up traffic. Concentrate on the driving. Oh, those terrible thoughts about his Julianna. Cora with her red hair, laughing, telling him a joke. Rosa yelling. Anything.

"You lived in Elko all your life?" Katy asked.

"No. Mainly Winnemucca. A few years in Battle Mountain. My mom worked in a turquoise shop there."

"We passed through there, didn't we?" Katy asked.

"Yes," said Sam.

The camper pulled in front of them. *If this camper's rockin', don't bother knockin'.*

Katy giggled and pointed, leaning slightly into the boy as she did so. George snorted a short laugh.

Again, the heat rose in Sam's face. This could not go on. He was going to have to think of some way to get these kids out of his car. Something was wrong, like a spirit, or a ghost. Something pricking away at his past, his memories. His conscience. If he could get them into Winnemucca, he would tell Katy. No more. Can't do any more.

What if they wouldn't let him go? Silly. How could they hold him? If he had to get the pistol out of the glove compartment. . . . Crazy thoughts. They weren't gangsters.

Katy rearranged the jacket on her lap. Sam was afraid to look at her, at the kid, at this George. Katy's lap was covered by the jacket. She turned a little on her side, away from Sam, resting her face against the back of the seat. Sam could not see George's hands now. He looked out the window. He had to wait an appropriate time in order to pass the camper. Hell. Forty-five miles an hour. He would never get anywhere at that rate. Cut the daydreaming. Out and around the camper. The man in the cowboy hat would think he was toying with him. *See-saw Margery Daw,/Jacky shall have a new master.* Now he remembered nursery rhymes. He must have sung that to his baby. See-saw. Sixty.

Katy wiggled in the seat next to him, and Sam saw that the boy's eyes were closed, his face toward Katy. He was pretending to sleep. Sam was convinced.

His hand had to be under that jacket. There was no other way to read it. Katy sighed. This damned kid's hand was up under her skirt. Sam was certain, and he could feel the flesh himself, feel it soft and giving, feel her moving to open for him, feel the hair and the sticky wetness. As if it was his hand, and his finger, and she moved accommodatingly. Sam was burning up, and he rubbed his eye too hard, wounding himself.

Katy's head slipped lower on the seat, more toward the boy, as if she were going to put her face in his lap.

George opened his eyes. He looked startled.

Sixty-five. Sam saw George's hands come up to Katy's shoulders, and he saw him look at her. He could not see Katy's face. The young man touched her, and the rage in Sam exploded in his chest, and the words caught and tumbled over each other, and nothing came out but a choking cough.

Don't touch her, his mind screamed, and he could feel Katy's body against him, feel her bare shoulders as if he touched her, straightened her in the seat himself.

"Boy, she's out like a light," George whispered. "Must be plenty tired. Thought she was going to fall on me."

Lying, Sam thought. Lying. She's not asleep. Pretending, tricking him. Soon they would be screwing in the back among the cases of concentrate, and he wanted to cry. He felt the tears burning his eyes. Christ, she was a baby. Hadn't Rosa said, she was a baby. A little girl and this kid with the hands and the muscular arms . . .

Sam could not see her face. He reached out and touched her hair. He expected her to turn and he thought he might see the face of Julianna, just for a second, and her hair was suddenly electric at his fingertips, and he drew his hand away, blinded, dumb.

"She's sick," he said. "I don't know what's wrong with her."

They don't know what's wrong with her. They think it might be a brain tumor. God, we hope it's not that. Sick, don't know what's wrong with her. Long distance to his sister on the farm, the farm he should have left before he did. He thought she would tell him everything was going to be all right, but she did not. And it wasn't, after all, not in the end.

"Maybe the flu. Where'd you pick her up?" George asked.

The young man did not sound accusing, the way Johnny and Rosa had done. Pick her up? What? She's mine, leave her alone. Sam pulled out around a blue sedan with such a sharp motion that he had to struggle to right the car straight into the lane.

"Wendover." He spoke so low in his throat, George could barely hear. Seventy. "Just outside Wendover. She asked me for a ride. She lives not too far . . ."

Ah, daughter, daughter. He stared at the car as he passed and looked directly into the eyes of the man who had stopped alongside the road. The child in the sunsuit was waving at him from the back seat. The woman faced straight ahead. He cut rapidly in front of them and pushed the accelerator nearly to the floor. There was a slight rise ahead, and the station wagon kicked into passing gear, and the angle was enough to seem to be pointed toward the sky. In the rearview mirror, he could see the blue sedan diminishing, the driver's face invisible behind the glare on the windshield. In the distance, he could see black thunderclouds forming, and he prayed for the rain, the noise of it battering against the car and blocking his vision, cutting him off from the man in the blue sedan and the grinning cowboy in the camper. He needed crashing thunder to lead him home.

Katy slumped against George, and he gently eased her down to his shoulder. Then he turned and looked out the back window.

"Hey," he said to Sam in a loud voice. "Hey, aren't you going to pull over?"

And in the mirror, when his shaking eyes looked there, Sam could see the red and white and blue huzzah of the highway patrol. Then the siren. Too late to avoid the siren.

Feeling every muscle of his body burning and tight,

Sam slowed and pulled the station wagon off the freeway onto the shoulder.

"You must have been going eighty-five," George said softly.

Katy sat up and rubbed her eyes.

Sam could see the patrolman getting out of his car. He came, book in hand, toward them.

Sam got out. He did not want the patrolman at the window. He did not want to sit and have the man with his damned dark glasses, his unrevealed eyes, quizzing him, chastising him, in front of George and Katy. The sound of the siren reverberated in his head, ringing, accusing, finding him out. They met at the right rear bumper of the station wagon, and Sam had his wallet in his hand, ready to identify himself before the patrolman could demand it.

The patrolman ran his tongue over his teeth as he looked at Sam's license.

"Speed limit's fifty-five," he said.

When he spoke, Sam noticed the man had an annoying twitch in his shoulder, as if he were stiff, had a kink in his neck. Sam stared past the man into the desert.

"Sorry," Sam muttered. He shook his head. He saw George and Katy watching him, and he sighed and leaned against the station wagon.

"Those your kids in the car?" the patrolman asked. His voice sounded hollow.

My daughter, Sam started to say, then changed his mind. He could feel the heat of the sun, and his face burned as if he were the target of it.

"My son and his girl friend," he lied.

"What's the hurry?" the patrolman asked. Again, the slight twitch of the shoulder.

"I've been driving this road for years. Forgot about the new law, I guess," Sam said. All those years of unlimited speed, straight empty roads.

"The law's not so new anymore," the patrolman said.

What the hell did he want? Did he expect Sam to get down on his knees and plead forgiveness?

"No excuse. All right?" Sam said.

The man looked up at Sam. He rubbed his chin with his finger as if he were undecided about something. The enormity of the lie hit Sam. What if the patrolman were to ask for identification from George and Katy? What the hell would he think if he found out Sam lied?

"You were exceeding by thirty miles an hour," the man said.

Sam could not think of anything else to say. He shook his head. The heat was beginning to make him sick. The heat and the fear. Why had he involved himself with the kids in the car? He could have told the girl he didn't take riders. It was true. He did not. All those years on the road; no riders.

"I see it's your birthday," the man said.

"Right."

"Too bad to get a ticket on your birthday."

Was he mocking him? He could not see the damned man's eyes. In the desert, in the sun, the eyes were always hidden.

"I need to see your registration," the patrolman added, flipping back the pages of his booklet.

Registration. Glove box. Back to the station wagon to the expectant stares of Katy and George. He walked along the side of the car. He slipped in the gravel and braced himself against the hot metal door.

He opened it without looking at either George or Katy. They sat silently, stiff in the seat as if they were afraid to breathe. Sam could feel it, the tension, and he wanted to shout, but could not even think of words to curse. He snapped open the glove box, and pulled the registration from a plastic packet. He was so hot he could feel the hair on his arms bristling, could feel his face drying, stiffening in the glare. The patrolman, cool in his khaki clothes, waited for him. Sam had to be careful not to slam the car door with enough impact to break the damned desert quiet with a crack.

"How fast was he going?" Katy asked George.

"He must have been doing over eighty," George said. "Probably still mad about what happened at Johnny's."

"What happened?" Katy asked, and turned to look at Sam. He stood waiting at the rear of the station wagon. The patrolman had returned to his own car. Sam stood with his back to them. He stubbed at the gravel with his shoe. He squinted at the glare from the windshield of the police car.

The patrolman spoke into a microphone.

George turned to look at Sam. He shook his head.

"My aunt and her big mouth," he said.

"Why don't you roll down your window," Katy asked. "It's suffocating in here."

George rotated the handle and leaned back against the seat. Katy studied him. His skin was olive, shiny and smooth. Dark hair, dark eyes. Odd, she thought. He looks like Sam.

"What did she say to him?"

"Rosa thinks every man is about to run away with some young chick," George said. "If my uncle had any sense, he would."

"Did they say something about me?"

"Rosa just goes on. You know."

"I'll bet he didn't like that." Katy was afraid to hear. Maybe he *was* going to leave her. He said he wasn't, but maybe, if she hadn't come running right then, right at that instant, he would have.

"Out there with a girl young enough to be your daughter," George said, mimicking his aunt's accent. He shook his head in disgust.

Katy felt the color rise in her face. So that was it. And she'd had those thoughts about Sam. She turned around again. The patrolman was writing out the ticket. "It's nothing like that," she whispered.

"So Rosa, she keeps right on poking at him, and finally he looks at her and says, 'My daughter's dead.' You should have seen Rosa's face."

George turned away from Katy, and scanned the sprawling desert on his right. "I decided I'd had enough of that."

Why hadn't Sam told her? Why had he lied? He could have said that his daughter had died so she would have understood. What if she had said something to hurt his feelings?

"When did his daughter die?" Katy asked. She placed her palms on her stomach. *I can take care of my daughter.*

"Pretty recently, I guess," George said. "So I figured I would go on over to Louie's place in Winnemucca. Who needs Rosa?"

Daughter. Was she a little girl? "How old was she?" Katy asked.

George shook his head.

"What did she die of?"

"I didn't hear."

Sam opened the door of the station wagon and got in. The highway patrol car pulled out around him and onto the road. He sat for a moment; then, with a set motion, a slight wince as he turned the ignition, he started the engine and without saying anything, pulled back onto the highway. There were red patches up the sides of his neck and around his ears.

It was unbearably hot in the car. The little streamers attached to the air-conditioning vent hung straight down. No cool air circulated to relieve the passengers. Sam's face was all red now, and he was perspiring in large clear drops. He stared ahead at the road, his face rigid.

Katy watched him, her hands folded tightly in her lap. A daughter. She imagined a little girl lying in the street, run down by a car. A street in Albany with small neat houses and well-kept lawns. She imagined Sam crying over a small coffin. Awful. A daughter who had died. She had never known a child who had died. She thought of her brothers playing kickball in the street just off the Arlington. Daughter. Dead. No wonder he seemed so upset. He didn't seem old enough to have someone die. She wanted to tell him she was sorry, but instead, because it was so terribly hot, she asked him if she could turn on the air conditioner.

Sam's concentration broke, and he looked at the control panel.

"Who turned it off?" he asked. "It should be on."

He slid the levers, looking alternately at them and at the road. He punched the knob that controlled the blower in and out. Nothing.

"God dammit," he said, hitting the dashboard with his hand. He stopped. He took a breath. "It's broken," he said. "This is a brand-new car, and the damned thing is broken."

"Do you want me to try it?" George asked, leaning over Katy toward the panel.

"You think you've got some magic touch?" Sam was furious. "Roll down the window."

"Sorry," George said, and he leaned back. He stared out the side window as he lowered it. He tipped his head slightly to catch the oncoming air in his face.

The air that rushed in was as hot as ever. Katy rubbed her arms, then refolded her hands. She had to say something, anything. She wanted to tell Sam she was sorry. He would relax and say it was all right. He would appreciate the sympathy. He would stop gripping the steering wheel so tightly, and he would lean back and sigh. She would be very gentle.

And then she saw her own parents. Her mother was crying uncontrollably; her father looked deathly pale. They stood by the side of a coffin, suffering the torments of the guilty.

"You were the one that wanted her to go away," Katy's mother said.

"You never loved her enough," Katy's father replied.

Then there were two more coffins, and they belonged to Katy's brothers.

"All of them gone," her grandmother said accusingly, shaking her head. Katy's mother fainted and no one rushed to help her. No one at all. Her father turned his back on his wife and walked away.

"Mr. Batinovich?" she whispered. "I'm really sorry about your daughter. George told me. What happened to her?"

Oh, it was too much, too much to tolerate. His Julianna, white in the white bed, bottles and clear tubes, dripping drops of glucose, transparent into transparent veins. Veins that could barely be traced. Searching, prodding, screaming. What happened? WHAT HAPPENED? Dying, dying. Doctors in white coats. Rosa, Rosa, Rosa, accusing. Thelma, accusing. The patrolman with the twitch in his shoulder, accusing. The man in the desert silhouetted, white sand blazing in the background, the sun blinding him, everything blinding him. White, white dead, and dying. WHAT HAPPENED? *Daddy, Daddy, come on.* The little girl in the sunsuit, running, running, running, up and down the ramp. Julianna, running, running, dying, dying. Footsteps in the hall. She can't come back. Running doctors in white coats. Nothing, nothing. Drops of glucose steadily dripping, ringing in his ears, ringing, shrieking, the sound of a siren and a flashing red light.

Sam hit the brakes. The station wagon skidded, rear wheels catching in the barrow pit. The wheels ground in the gravel; the brakes screamed. He heard Katy gasp. He could feel the terror as he struggled to get the car straight and off the road. The sun and the white and the sound whirled by him, and he thought they would certainly roll over, glass would shatter, children, whose children? would cry and wail. Someone would moan.

Then, as if caught by a giant hand, the station wagon stopped abruptly, throwing Katy forward into the dashboard. George pulled her back, scraping her neck as he reached for her.

"You'll have to get out," Sam said. "Both of you." Sorry, sorry, sorry, words running together, unspoken.

They did not understand. He could see, though his eyes trembled, they had no idea. The girl put her hand to her forehead. She stared at him, confused. She brought her hand down, looked dazedly at her fingers and the sticky blood, then tried to shake it away.

"Okay, okay," George said to Sam as he opened the door. He pulled at Katy.

"Wait," Sam stammered. "You see, there is a pain in my head." His hand moved to his own forehead, but it was Katy that was bleeding. It was Julianna's head that ached, her poor head, large on the pillow, her head with the circle of dull pain that she touched with feeble fingers.

"Come on," George said. "Katy, get out." He scrambled in back of her for the packs.

Blood ran into Katy's eyes, and she brushed it away like rain.

"I'm sorry," she cried. "Really . . ."

Sam covered his face with his hands and slumped over the steering wheel. He gripped the hard-ridged wheel until he thought his knuckles would split.

"Katy," George said, "is this all your stuff? Hey, look, help me out, okay?" He grabbed her shoulders and turned her to him. He groaned at the sight of the bloodied face. One trickle of blood down the side of her face had met and joined with another from the scratch at her throat.

"Someone else will give you a ride," Sam muttered.

George tried to move Katy, but her arms were rigid, and she did not seem to know where she was. It was hotter than ever, the white gravel throwing heat up at them, the sun burning from above.

Sam spoke through dry sobs. "Get out, please . . ."

George succeeded in getting Katy from the car. Her sunglasses slipped from her lap into the gravel. She held on to George, groping in the brightness, her feet sliding on the rocks.

"It's all right," George said, but his voice was shaky.

Katy put her hand to her forehead, and her fingers came away bloody again.

"My head hurts," she wailed.

George slammed the door of the station wagon. Katy's pack rolled down into a small ditch by the road, and George led her down the incline. His tee shirt was stained with her blood; he pulled his shirt away from his body and looked at it.

In a sudden burst of anger, he turned back to the station wagon and screamed at Sam. "She's hurt, damn you. Can't you see, she's hurt?"

He saw Sam push himself away from the wheel, and he heard the grinding sound of the ignition. He saw Sam wipe at his face, and his eyes with his hand, and then thrust the station wagon into gear.

Katy and George were lucky to be down away from the road. The gravel flew in all directions. The tires skidded until Sam was able to catch the pavement and get away.

George watched the station wagon disappear into the stream of traffic. Two motorcycles pulling small white trailers passed them by. So did a Volkswagen bus and a red Volvo, with a whistle in the manifold, carrying four people from Delaware. A Nevada telephone company truck with a wire-loaded spool in the back went by without pausing.

George watched until he could no longer tell which car belonged to Sam. He glared as if he could punish the man with his eyes.

"I'll tell my father," Katy cried. "I will."

George took her by the shoulders and looked into her confused eyes.

"Tell him what?"

"Tell him the joke."

"The joke?" He did not understand.

She sobbed and clung to him while he tried to figure out how to clean the cut on her forehead, how to get them a ride into Winnemucca, and how to keep them from being broiled alive in the damned desert sun of his glorious home state.

The tightness in Sam's jaw made his teeth ache. He gripped the steering wheel, rubbing the hard plastic with his thumbs. He stared straight ahead through the remnants of tears and tried to forget Katy's face and the blood that trickled down into her eye.

Why had she asked? Why couldn't she have just let it go? Every question did not deserve an answer. *What happened?* He smiled painfully. "Why is the sky blue?" Julianna asked. "Where did Cindy's mother go after she died?" "Why am I your little girl instead of somebody else's?"

And why, he wondered, would God give a fourteen-year-old girl a brain tumor. The Georges and Katys would go right on, protected. Katy's head was bleeding. He had never seen so much as a drop of blood on Julianna's face. But now, he could not remember. The faces merged. Tears rose in his eyes again. Would he ever look at another girl without thinking of his daughter? Without remembering his own arousal? How long could this go on?

Sam could not remember how he stopped the station wagon. George had shouted at him, but he could not recall what. His head ached with a wide band of tension, and he touched his face with a gentle finger. He would have to forget it. He would never see either one of them again. Katy with her face streaming blood, Julianna with her hair falling out on the pillow.

He had to concentrate on the speed. Fifteen years since he had a ticket. He'd felt like such a fool. George and Katy had acted as if they expected him to be carted away in handcuffs. No excuse. None. Eighty-five miles an hour.

Though the sky was darker now, the clouds rolling toward him, the air in the station wagon was still unbearably hot. Sam ran one hand through his hair, feeling the perspiration on his scalp. He was still shaking. He saw a sharp thread of lightning in the distance, golden and fine and quick. A storm wouldn't cool the desert completely, but it would help.

If he could forget George and Katy . . .

To the northwest, the sky was coal-smoke black along the low mountains. Another bolt of lightning gave the illusion of going straight from the eye of the cloud to the earth. The smell of impending rain quickened his senses. He started to say "please" aloud, then stopped, bewildered by the impulse. In his mind, he heard a girl's scream. Katy, falling to the ground.

There was no reason to think about going back. Someone must have picked them up by now.

When he was a child, he had been afraid of the fierce Montana electrical storms. There was one every afternoon in summer. The clouds would swarm out of the Yellowstone range, cover the sky above Red Lodge, and the lightning would arc from one plateau to another, crossed and joined, thunder overlapping one strike, then another. Often the clatter of hail accompanied the storm thunder, completely enveloping the valley in noise and fragmented light and dark.

He had, one day when his mother was away and his

father out in the fields, forced himself to stand in the middle of the yard. Not under a tree, he was smarter than that. He had stood out there in the open space and let the lightning and thunder crash about him, the drenching rain blinding him and hiding his tears. He stood there until he was over his fear, long enough to prove that the lightning was not going to kill him.

So that now, he greeted the smell of coming rain, the dark clouds, the layers moving swiftly above his head, with his chin thrust out, forward, into the eye of the storm.

And he wondered what had given him, that day when he was eleven or twelve, the courage to stand there. What had driven him to face it? He could, as he remembered, feel the first big drops of rain on his face. After all those years, he could feel the danger in the pit of his stomach.

And, he thought bitterly, it might have been his bravest moment.

There was another streak of lightning, and this time, an overhead flash that illuminated a large area. A swell of thunder overcame the noise of the engine, and the first drop of rain splattered against the windshield. Sam shifted in the seat. Another drop spreading to a circle three inches in diameter. He thought of Katy and George standing by the side of the road.

Soon the drops were coming fast, striking the glass in regular cadence. Sam waited until he could not see the road at all before he turned on the windshield wipers. From the half-open window, rain sprayed the side of his face, cooling him. Rain splattered the seat where George had been sitting, making shiny circles on the upholstery.

If he could just get to Kristo's, he could sit in his office and watch the rain splash against the bright neon bulbs of the Star Broiler Cafe and Casino across the street. Kristo would light his pipe, and Sam would have a drink. If he could just forget about George and Katy standing in the rain.

He brushed at the water on his face, and when he looked at his hand he expected to see blood. A stream of red on Katy's face. Eyes filled with confusion and pain. Whose eyes? Julianna's, Katy's, Cora's, his own. The rain cracked against the windshield with such force he was afraid the glass would break.

He could not stand it any longer. He would have to go back. The rain could strike them down, the lightning annihilate them in the desert. He peered through the flashing wipers, through the gray drops, and he could not see any place to turn around. He would have to risk cutting across the low dirt and gravel ravine that divided the highway. He could not see anything behind him. Pressing the brakes nearly to the floor, he turned into the dirt. He hit a clump of sagebrush, dragging it with him. He hoped to hell the highway patrol was not any-where near. He had to get back. He'd left too many people unprotected. He must stop it, stop it now.

He skidded in the wet dirt and gravel; he pressed the accelerator, and the rear of the station wagon slipped, but the tires caught and propelled him up onto the high-way. A truck, horn blaring, swerved and went by him, throwing rainwater from the road at him like a wave of pellets. Another car, headlights glaring through the rain, appeared dangerously close, and he pulled into the other lane, cursing, his words nearly obliterated by another cloud-splitting clap of thunder.

He took a series of deep breaths in order to calm himself. He planned what he would say to them, how he would explain. He would ask them to forgive him; it wouldn't hurt him to do that. The smell of rain-dampened clothes, the chatter of words, of relief, of gratitude. Sorry, sorry, sorry. He must be near the place. If only he could see more clearly. A hill coming up on the left. Just the other side of that, he was certain.

He prayed, without understanding that he did so, his lips silently forming the words, that they would be there waiting for him to return.

They stood, two small figures against the vast Nevada landscape. They stood while cars sped by them and George tried to comfort Katy.

"He could have killed us," George muttered as he held Katy in his arms. "What the hell did he do that for?"

"I shouldn't have asked him about his daughter," she sobbed. "He'd been so nice to me, helped me, and I upset him." She moved her hand once again to her forehead and the cut.

Just as they heard the first rumble of thunder, a car stopped beside them. The woman rolled down the window and said in a precise voice, "This time, it looks like you need our help."

Katy blinked. Blue sedan. A little girl peered from the back window. She waved at Katy.

"Come ride in our car," she said, her curly hair short, strawberry blond. "Come ride with us."

"Thanks," George said, and pulled Katy toward the car.

"No," Katy whispered. "I don't . . ."

"It's all right," George said, patiently.

"I don't want to ride . . ."

"Get in the car," George said as the woman leaned forward, pulling up the seat so Katy could enter.

The man, who was by then out from behind the steering wheel, unlocked the trunk.

"Give me your packs," he said.

"No," Katy whimpered.

George shrugged and handed the packs to the man.

The first drops of rain smacked the windshield.

"Here's something to clean up your face," the woman said, and she passed a package of towelettes back to Katy. She handed them over her shoulder without turning to look at her.

Katy murmured, "Thank you."

The woman leaned forward and George got into the back seat with Katy.

The little girl stared at Katy's face and said, "You look bloody."

"We sure thank you for picking us up," George said.

The man got in, started the engine, and drove back onto the highway.

Katy rubbed the damp tissue against her aching head. She could not see. She had no mirror. She rubbed and dabbed absently at the spot.

"Did you see this lady's blood, Mommy?" the child asked.

"Yes. She hurt her head," the woman said.

"And her neck, too," said the little girl.

George turned and watched Katy's awkward movements. The blood had begun to dry, and it crusted in flakes on the side of her face. She had rubbed the cut in one place so hard it started to bleed again, and a small trickle ran down to her eyebrow.

"Just a minute," he said tenderly as he took one of the towelettes from her. As gently as he could, he cleaned away the blood. Katy closed her eyes.

"There," he said finally, and he lifted one of her hands. "Take this and hold it right on this spot."

Katy leaned back against the seat. The car swayed on the highway, smooth, humming in the rain.

"Can I sit on your lap?" the little girl asked Katy.

"Sure," Katy said, "if you really want to." She placed her hand on her stomach.

"Why don't you sit on my lap till Katy's head feels better," George volunteered.

"You come up here, Mary Ann," the woman said. "You come up here with me, right now."

"I want to sit on his lap," the child whined.

"You come here. Now." The woman left no room for dissent in her tcne.

And the child paid no attention to her mother. She sat with a determined plop on Katy's lap and put one arm around her neck. Katy forced a smile at the child's serious face.

"Your mommy wants you to get up front with her," Katy said.

"No," stated Mary Ann. Her baby-plump legs and arms were damp from the heat. Her sunsuit was wrinkled. She had bright pink spots on her shoulders where the sunburn had peeled away. Her hair was damp and curling around her forehead. She looked like a cherub with her rosy coloring. Unfortunately, she smelled faintly of urine, and her hands were sticky when she touched Katy's skin.

"We offered you help once before," the man said. "We aren't people who pass by, looking neither to the left nor to the right, like those who passed by before the Good Samaritan . . ."

"She sure is a cute little girl," George said, a false smile on his face.

"Mary Ann, I want you up here right now." The woman turned. She was angry, and she stared at the little girl. The woman's face was thin, and she had hard brown eyes. "I will count to three . . ."

"Come on, Mary Ann," George said.

"One," said the woman.

Mary Ann looked at Katy. She turned back to her mother and stared at her. She put her arm around Katy's neck and held her tighter.

"Two," said the woman.

"No," said Mary Ann.

For a moment there was just the sound of the rain and the hum of the engine.

"You better do what your mama says," Katy offered. She tried to pull Mary Ann's arms away from her neck. The child had irritated the scratch.

"Say something to your daughter," the woman said to the man.

"Mary Ann, you come up front. You can have an apple."

Mary Ann seemed to be thinking it over.

"Mary Ann, you get up here in front before your mother says 'three' or you know what will happen to you," the man added. He spoke in the same flat voice he used to Sam in the desert.

Mary Ann decided to get into the front seat. She knew the last second she could wait before the count of three. She stood up on the back seat and looked at Katy. Mary Ann leaned forward. She was going to give Katy a kiss on the cheek. Six inches from Katy's face, Mary Ann stuck out her tongue. With two of her chubby baby fingers, she pinched Katy's arm.

"I want to get in the front," she said, and turned her back to Katy. "Help me get into the front."

Katy started to speak, but in her astonishment, could not think of what to say. She looked at George. He had not seen the pinch. Mary Ann was bending over the seat, her bottom in the air, the white ruffled edge of her panties visible under the sunsuit. Her plump legs dangled, and Katy resisted the urge to pinch her little behind as hard as she could. Instead, Katy gave her a push and the child struggled into the front seat.

Once Mary Ann was settled down between her parents, the woman began to talk. She cut an apple into quarters and gave a piece to each of them. Mary Ann wanted a whole apple. She said so until she was handed one by her mother. A slap into the hand. Bright red apple.

The man and woman did not turn to look at George and Katy as they spoke. They sat straight in their seats.

"I don't want you to tell us in front of the child what the man did to you," the woman said.

"We have been watching you since Wendover," the man added.

"What are you talking about?" asked George.

"Not you. The girl," the man said.

"What do you mean, 'watching'?" George asked anyway.

"She was sick at the rest stop," the woman said. "Then she got into that station wagon with a strange man. You were asking for trouble, young lady, and that's exactly what you got."

Katy scowled out at the rain. It pounded on the windshield, large drops hitting clear in the middle, then splattering and running around the edges. The air filled with light, and above the hum of the engine came the thunder.

"He didn't do anything to hurt me," Katy said.

"We can sure see that," the man said, contempt in his voice.

"Are you a runaway?" the woman asked.

"No. I'm on my way home. My parents knew where I was. Colorado. I'm going home to Berkeley."

"When Christ comes again, meccas of sin like Berkeley will be in flames," the woman said. She turned and handed Katy another piece of apple.

"I don't think you understand," George said.

"Young man," the woman said, "you are the one who does not understand. There are evil people in the world."

George did not eat his piece of apple. He held it gingerly in his hand and examined it as if something might be the matter with it.

"We just want people to know. It is our duty to warn you." The man spoke more rapidly now, an edge of excitement in his voice. "So we can all be together in the kingdom of heaven."

Mary Ann stood on the front seat and stared at Katy and George. She rested her chin on her hands and looked at them. Katy was fascinated with her mouth. Any minute, Mary Ann would stick out her tongue again, but she would wait until she was positive that neither of her parents could see her. She took sharp little bites from her apple, and her eyes sparkled with a demonic glint.

The woman interrupted the man's speech. "You have to understand, before it is too late, that your sins, your earthly sins will bring eternal damnation to your souls."

George was wide-eyed at the dialogue. Every muscle in his body seemed tense. He looked at Katy with alarm.

And Mary Ann watched them.

"Man must assume his role again as head of the family; woman must redefine her duty in the home, caring for and loving her family, serving. The family must survive." The man smoothed his hair on the top of his head. He had very long slender fingers and his nails were almost white.

"It must start with you people, you young ones. You cause so much of the difficulty because you do not believe."

Katy sighed, folded and unfolded her hands and looked out at the foothills. Dark clouds hung over them, misting, moving, swirling quickly as if stirred by a large wire whip.

George looked plainly horrified. Without a glance, he reached out and took Katy's hand. Drops of perspiration formed on his face.

"He's touching her," Mary Ann announced. "He's holding her hand. I can see."

Katy started to pull away, then did not. She stared at the child that had once looked like a cherub and wanted to smack her fat little face.

The woman continued. "We are having drought, famine."

"Where are you from?" George had the courage to interrupt.

"North Carolina," the man said.

"You don't have any southern accent," George added.

"We are originally from Utah. We have been visiting there, and are now on our way to San Jose to see my sister," the woman said.

"We just need to go as far as Winnemucca, if you don't mind."

Katy thought George's voice shook. He still held her hand as if to signal her. He was saying, we will get out of this car at Winnemucca, come hell or high water, or fire and brimstone. He said it with a squeeze of the hand.

And Katy merely thought the people were odd.

"You young people would find the road through life much easier if you had religious guidance, that's for sure." The man reached for a piece of the apple.

"If you would put your faith in the Father, you would not find yourselves in the desert. God rewards. God punishes. That's all we can say to you."

"This is the last of the apples," the woman said. She gave everyone another quarter.

A sign read, END FREEWAY, ¼ MILE. KEEP TO THE RIGHT. The rain still pelted the windshield, but the side windows were almost clear. Katy leaned over and looked up at the sky. Layers of gray dark clouds floated ahead. Another flash of lightning, a roll of thunder, muffled but distinguishable.

SLOW TO 35. A few feet farther. 25 MILES PER HOUR SPEED LIMIT.

"Could you let us out in the middle of town?" George asked. "We're going to my cousin's place."

"All we ask in return is that you think about God and about your own salvation," the man said.

"We think the girl should ride with us to California," the woman reminded him. She talked as if Katy could not hear.

"Jesus wants me for a sunbeam," Mary Ann began to sing. "To shine for him each day. In every way try to please him, at home, at school, at play. A sun-beam, a sunbeam . . ." Child's voice, off-key, high innocence. Mary Ann clapped her hands and laughed.

"Sun-beam," she said and pointed at her little chest. "Me." She narrowed her eyes and stuck out her tongue.

"I'm going to stay in Winnemucca for a while, too," Katy said.

The street was lined with businesses. Motels and service stations along the road that curved into the town. Neon lights glimmered through the rain, and everything was gray and washed. The road was slick with water now, and the people ran with newspaper over their heads. Women wore plastic rain bonnets, the kind carried in a tiny pouch in a purse.

Summer rain. Cloudburst, wetting down all the dust. Making the grass bright garden green. Deceiving.

"Right there would be just great," George said, squeezing Katy's hand. The man pulled into a parking space in front of the Star Broiler and Cafe. The sidewalk in front was covered with a green felt carpet. A statue of an Indian, carved and painted wood, greeted them.

"Thank you," Katy managed to say as George helped her out of the car. The man opened the trunk and put their packs on the green sidewalk.

Katy and George stood together, blinking at the raindrops that fell into their eyes. They watched the blue sedan back out away from the curb and join the flow of traffic westward.

Mary Ann smiled innocently back at them and waved one small hand. "Bye," her lips formed, and she had the same odd cold look in her eyes.

There was another rumble of thunder, and Katy started to laugh. She doubled over, holding her stomach. "Can you believe them?" She giggled. "And that sweet little thing pinched me. A sunbeam. Wow."

When she saw George frowning, she stopped. "I'm sorry," she said without knowing why.

He shook his head. "Let's go," he said. "My cousin's place is just around the corner."

He walked ahead of her. She could not see his face. She hurried to catch up with him, touched his arm to slow his pace. She wanted to tell him how amazing it was to feel like they were old friends. She wanted to take his hand and hold it the way he had held hers in the car.

Around the corner and down the street, in the middle of the block, was the Pizza Place.

"That's it," George said, and Katy looked at him: "I think religious fanatics are dangerous," he added.

"But," Katy said, "what could they do to us?"

"We're getting soaked," he said. "Let's hurry."

Rain washed Katy's shoulders and feet. Her sandals squished when she walked, but at least it was cooler. A

flash of light and an immediate crash of thunder propelled them down the street. George looked at the sky,
then at Katy. He pushed open the swinging door of the
Pizza Place.

He had found the place; he was certain of that, and they were gone. Sam parked the station wagon off to the side of the road, and he sat with his head in his hands. There was no place for George and Katy to hide, no shelter they could have sought against the storm. The hill was barren except for low brush. Not a tree, not a cave, nothing. He knew someone had picked them up, and instead of being relieved, he was still terrified. The rain was less intense now, and made a simple sorrowful patter against the windshield.

He had to begin the retreat into Winnemucca; he had to forget about them. He checked the rearview mirror for oncoming traffic, and seeing that there was none, he pulled back onto the highway. He needed to concentrate on a steady safe speed, on restoring an evenness to his breathing. Someone had given them a ride. There was nothing else he could do. No way to explain to them, or to himself.

Accept it, he chanted. Accept. A car sped by him, and the water from the road once again smashed against the windshield, startling him. The rain was letting up, but just before he pulled into a clear blue space, a streak of lightning crossed the nearest dark cloud. Then, the rain stopped as abruptly as if he had driven into another room. A shaft of sunlight froze the water on the hood into brightly reflected drops.

The sky was huge, blue and black, the clouds layered in ascending levels, moving swiftly overhead. He could see the glistening cars and vans moving along. Brilliant reds and greens and blues. White whites, and shinier blacks, all glimmering beneath the bright funnel of light. And yet, ahead, he could see another dark bank of clouds, see the angry lines of lightning waiting.

And he thought as he drove toward Winnemucca, and Kristo's office, and the neon star, that the desert was a damned big place. The people and their machines were moving dots of color, tiny in the bowl where six kinds of weather could range at once, and he could see all of them. Two minuscule children, minuscule lives standing by the side of the road, waiting for another minute particle to rescue them. He needed that much room. He needed to see white and gray and black clouds, sunlight and rain, all of those things that went relentlessly on the way that life, his life, must.

He could not think about the unsaid words, the unresolved terrors. He would never have done anything to hurt his Julianna. He would not have entered her darkened bedroom in the night, pulled back the covers. No. He gripped the steering wheel and headed into the last storm front before Winnemucca. If she had lived, he would have been able to prove it to her. He would have watched her grow, blossom, and he would have loved her in a perfect rain-washed way. It would never have happened again, and he would be able to laugh about it.

And he would like to take Katy's hand, look into her eyes and say, it had nothing to do with you, sweetheart. It was my grief. That's all. Now he would never see Katy and George again. His life seemed to be filled with people he could not find, people to whom he would never be able to apologize.

He was under the darkness once again, and the sun was gone. The rain returned. A few big drops first, then the steady torrent. The contours of the vast Nevada land were hidden from him, and he was alone. No one whispered secrets into his ear.

The speed-limit signs announced the approach of Winnemucca, and Sam sighed with relief. He recognized the businesses, the motels, the cafes, the stores. Signposts that did not change except that the sun faded their colors; the rain swept them bright again. Kristo, a drink, a talk. Comfort in the way things used to be. Why did he feel as if a stranger, like a ghost, stood between him and his home? Between him and his wife. He wanted to touch her, to make love to her, and he was afraid he might kill her with his passion. A man with hands too large to hold a violet.

Then, as he drove and just as he least expected it, there was another flash of light, and a boom of cracking thunder. He shuddered at the incongruity of it all. Violet stems, smoke, light, color, space, and time. And in the midst of it all, a memory like a black volcanic cloud.

He wished it was as simple as forgiveness, as simple as the whispered words of love.

PART TWO

By the time Sam entered Kristopoulis's restaurant, he had managed to convince himself that the events of the day had simply collided in his head and in his heart like the masses of air that produced the thunder and lightning. Too much bad news to have to give in one day, his birthday on top of it all. It wasn't anyone's fault. Not his, not Katy's. He attached his thoughts to details, trivial things that would help him forget what had happened.

Kristo was going to be able to joke him out of the panic. He would soothe, no question about it. Kristo was an even man, a man who had been born of poor immigrant people and who now had a brick and flagstone house outside of town. A house surrounded with trees, a blue swimming pool, and a Cadillac in the garage. Sam could have a couple of drinks, a conversation, then be on his way. The rain would clear the air. He would stay overnight in Reno, then see his customers there in the morning. Maybe pick up a new one. Be home by tomorrow night. Little late, but what did it matter. He could get there by six if Thelma had planned a dinner for his birthday. He could forget about Katy. A nice dinner. Thelma had paid more attention to the cooking. New cookbooks. More time. She talked about getting a job, but he had not encouraged her. Maybe that was wrong.

She might invite the neighbors, friends for fifteen years. Sam and Thelma had moved into their house when Julianna was a baby. A little house, but Sam had added a nice family room. Fireplace, carpet, nice comfortable furniture. They lived in that room. A family. A platform rocker, a color television set, a collection of books on the Civil War. Kristo had given Sam a book on Greek art once, and Sam read it all the way through. He and Julianna had looked at the pictures of famous statues, and when she studied Michelangelo in school, he bought her an expensive book on the artist. He had intended to buy her more. He wanted her to know things that he did not. Now the two books were side by side in the case near the fireplace. Thelma suggested they take an art appreciation course, but he had been reluctant. He thought the art belonged to Julianna.

Kristo's Restaurant-Casino-Bar was the second largest in Winnemucca. Sam pushed open the swinging glass doors and entered the casino. The room was filled with slot machines and colored lights. Red and orange carpeting muted the sound of footsteps, and overhead lights spotted each machine. He smiled. He was not a gambler. He'd spent too much time traveling in Nevada to need to pump his money into the slots. Eventually, everyone lost, he thought. An old lady in a navy blue dress with white dots stood at the nickel machine. She scowled at Sam as he passed, and he scowled back. She pulled the handle and stared at the whirling fruit.

Gamblers amused him. There were all kinds in a casino like this one. Young, sweet-looking things with cowboys saying, "Honey, you just put in your dime and pull this little handle and whoopee, some money will roll right out into your little hand." Or a crotchety housewife with the change from the supermarket standing there with rollers in her hair and rubber beach shoes on her damned old feet.

The ancient black man, with what looked like a coat of white dust on his skin, stood at the dime machine. His shoulders were stooped, and his eyes dull next to the shiny symbols of luck.

At the blackjack tables in the daytime were the serious players. They were the ones with hard looks on their faces, no expression in the eyes. The dealer Sam passed on his way to Kristo's office spent most of his time looking over the tops of the slightly bowed heads out into the maze of slot machines hoping, Sam supposed, for a glimpse of beauty.

And he thought there was something about casino light that did not seem to flatter people, but then after all, they weren't there to look at each other. They were there to hear the bells ring and the money pour forth into a bucket.

He walked past the empty bandstand and the dance floor, and opened the door marked PRIVATE. He walked up narrow carpeted stairs. At the top was another closed door. He knocked.

"Yes?"

Kristo was there. Sam sighed with relief.

"Sam Batinovich. Open up in the name of the law."

Sam could hear the man laughing, and he opened the door and stuck his head inside Kristo's office.

"Not doing anything indecent in here are you, Kristo?"

"Come on in, Sam," the man said, and leaned back in his chair. "It's been a long time."

Peter George Kristopoulis sat behind his large walnut desk, a successful man in a shiny well-cut gray suit. Once, when he and Sam walked through the casino, a blond woman in a blue dress had come up to them. She had a martini in her hand, and her neck was wrinkled although she did not look old.

"This here your brother?" she had winked at Kristo. "He looks like your brother. He looks just like you." She had wavered slightly, leaning closer to Sam, the martini dripping clear from the glass onto the carpet. "Hell, he looks like your goddamned twin."

"Yes, Lucille, this man is my brother," Kristo had said, putting his arm around Sam. "If a Yugoslav and a Greek can be brothers, then surely he is mine."

Sam sat down in the black overstuffed chair that faced Kristo's desk.

"What can I get you?" Kristo asked, reaching for the intercom on his desk.

"Well, you old devil," Sam said, looking at Kristo's smooth tan face. "It's my goddamned birthday so it better be something good."

Kristo laughed, his eyes narrowing for a minute, then he grinned broadly at Sam.

"Yes?" came the squeaky response of the intercom.

"Tell Shirl to bring up a bottle of champagne, two glasses. A plate of meatballs, some feta, bread, a tray . . ."

"You twenty-one?" Kristo smiled and turned off the intercom.

"Right. Just old enough to drink and whore." The words sounded odd to him. His ease was faltering and he hoped Shirl would be quick with the champagne.

"I know you're up on the supplies, but I thought I'd stop by." Sam wondered how he was going to keep up this kind of conversation. He saw Katy's face again, the blood trickling into her eye. She stared at him, the blank glazed look of the dead. Silver.

"You don't look so good, Sam. You feeling okay?" Kristo leaned forward over the desk. His voice was concerned, his look compassionate. Sam felt his face warm, his breath shorten.

"I must have the old-man blues."

Kristo snorted. "You're not old enough for the old-man blues. *I* am old enough. Not you. I know how old you are, Sam Batinovich. I've got an excellent memory for birthdays, and you told me once. You are forty-one on this day. I am fifty-eight. Forty-one is nothing compared to fifty-eight." He roared with laughter.

The door opened and a waitress came in with the champagne. She had long brown hair, and Sam thought she looked a little like a country singer. Something familiar about her. She smiled at Sam, but was obviously surprised to see him.

Kristo winked at him. "Shirl here expected you to be someone else. The champagne, you see. Fifty-eight is not all the way over the hill."

The woman was not a young girl. Not like Katy. She was thirty, maybe thirty-five. Katy, standing by the road, her head bleeding, the rain pouring down.

While Kristo opened the champagne, and the woman went back for the food, Sam walked to the window and looked through the venetian blinds. Across the street, the Star Broiler and Casino blinked yellow lights at him. The giant neon words twinkled, and Sam shook his head.

"Here's to you, Sam," Kristo said, and Sam turned to take a glass of champagne from him.

"Thanks." Sam felt awkward with the delicately stemmed glass in his hand. Violets. He could not remember the last time he'd had champagne. A wedding, he supposed, but he could not remember whose it was. A lady's drink, he thought. Odd, for two men. Maybe he would get a bottle for Thelma.

"And to all those things we old men have yet to experience." Kristo nodded and sipped from his glass.

The rain still ran gray against the window. Kristo seemed to be reflecting on something in his own life, as if Sam were a messenger for his own memories.

"You know, Sam," Kristo said, "next month, I'm going to Europe. For the first time, I'm going."

"Good for you," Sam said. "It's about time."

Kristo waved one hand toward the bookshelves that lined one wall of his office.

"You know, all these years, I've been reading those books, studying those pictures, wanting to see the sculpture, to touch that white marble, wanting to get up close to paintings done by men like Van Gogh, Titian. Now, I'm going to go. Alone. Helen, she doesn't want to travel, says her health isn't good enough. And, I don't know, Sam . . ." He paused and took another sip of the champagne. "I wonder if I really should do it."

"You better go ahead," Sam said abruptly. Should he tell Kristo about death? Should he tell him about Julianna and how suddenly things could change and there were no second chances? Dammit, he better not wait. No one seemed to have any time. No one had time! "You've been planning it, wanting to go, I mean. You *should* go. You owe it to yourself."

"But do I? I wonder," Kristo said.

"Hell, you've got plenty of money," Sam said.

"I know."

"I don't see the problem."

"Ah," Kristo sighed, "but you know, what if it's not as good as my dreams?" He smiled at Sam. "Like beautiful women. Sometimes they are not, upon closer scrutiny, what they seem."

Sam finished the champagne in his glass and looked out the window at the street. He saw a girl that looked like Katy, but it was not. She's on her way home, he thought. Safe.

"It's still raining," he said. "Long lasting storm for this damned desert."

"Things are changing, Sam. The weather, everything."

Shirl came in with a plate of cheese and lettuce, dolma, meatballs, and bread. She wore a short black skirt and a red off-the-shoulder blouse. She put the platter on Kristo's desk. Sam stared at her legs, and when he looked up, she was smiling at him.

"You two sure do look alike," she said.

"I'm his uncle," Kristo laughed. "Isn't that so, Sam? Two old devils, drinking in the middle of the day."

"Don't be silly," she said, and adjusted the shoulder of her blouse, pulling at the elastic as if it bothered her delicate skin. "You two? Old?"

"You can see why I've got Shirl around here, can't you?" Kristo said. "Shirl always knows the right thing to say."

Sam wanted to touch the woman's shoulders. He wanted to put his large hands right there and slide that blouse all the way off her shoulders and look at her bare breasts. He turned back to the window. He could imagine the woman naked. But then blood trickled down her body, and she was gone, and he could not trace the wound, did not know what made her bleed.

"Call me if you want anything else, boys," Shirl said as she left the office.

"You going to stay the night?" Kristo asked.

"No. I should go on to Reno."

"Too bad. I got a new act in the lounge. Belly dancer. Macedonian band. You'd like that, Sam. We could have a birthday party."

The rain was no longer pounding the windowpanes. The sun was out, and the raindrops glistened on the glass. Far away, there was another slight rumble of thunder, then nothing.

"The belly dancer," Kristo laughed. "Helen, she didn't like the idea. I explained to her. 'It is symbolic,' I said. 'It is the symbol of Mother Earth giving birth—that's what belly dancing is. Giving birth.' " Kristo laughed. " 'You are disgusting,' she said. Helen doesn't come to the club anymore. It's her health."

Sam looked at his empty glass. "Where the hell did you get a Macedonian band in these parts?" he asked.

"I hired one from Berkeley, California, where else?"

"And I should stay overnight in Winnemucca to hear a band from Berkeley?" Sam smiled.

"And see the belly dancer give birth to the world, don't forget that," Kristo answered.

Sam looked out the window again. Puddles on the street threw bright sprays of water as cars drove through them. The traffic headed west under a partial rainbow, splashed like a broken arch against the sky.

"There's a rainbow," Sam said.

"But there isn't a pot of gold," Kristo replied.

"Is everything a myth? Belly dancers giving birth to the world, pots of gold?" Sam squinted at the sun. He decided he would stay in Winnemucca. He deserved a birthday party. Kristo deserved a trip.

Kristo stood from his desk. "I've got a new book, Sam. Let me show you. Yes, everything's a myth. But let me show you a picture of a statue that I will see next month. It's in Florence, Italy. *Firenze*. I have been practicing." He went to the shelves and took down a volume of art reproductions. "The Medici Chapel. Yes." He turned the pages slowly. "Dawn, Dusk . . . see?"

Thunderheads shadowed the sky, weakening the light of day. Still, when George opened the door, a triangle of light fell on the dark floor of the Pizza Place. Katy touched her head as if her injury instead of the dim light was responsible for her poor vision. She squinted. Two men sat at the long bar.

"Come on," George said as she hesitated. "This is it."

The restaurant was dark and warm, moist-smelling from the rain. Small red lamps were attached to the walls. They glowed in an isolated row. Katy touched her hand to George's back so she would not trip over an unseen object in front of her. He walked directly to the seated men.

The mirror reflected the red lights, and glasses sparkled, indistinct forms. It was difficult to tell where one began and the other left off. Bottles of liquor lined the glass shelves. Katy saw a tall yellow decanter of Galliano as she walked behind George. Harvey Wallbangers. Four of them. To loosen her up, Kurt had said.

"I can't see," she whispered. She looked at the faces of the men. They stared straight ahead into the mirror.

"Louie around?" George asked.

There were wooden tables with straight-backed chairs.

Near the wall, the chairs were still piled upside down on top of long tables. Katy rubbed her forehead again. The furniture was old, mismatched, shadowy. A pinpoint of light came through a three-cornered tear in the drapes, and it was impossible not to be drawn to the spot.

"Hey, Louie," one man shouted. "Somebody wants you."

A rumble of thunder rattled the windowpanes. The glasses, row on row, glistened and sent small beams of light in patches of white around the bar.

The door from the kitchen swung open, and Katy turned in time to see a young man jump into the room. His hair was tied back away from his face with a blue bandanna, Indian style. Over his jeans and T-shirt, he wore an apron tied tightly around his waist.

"Somebody wants me," he sang, "I wonder who, I wonder who he can be . . ." He sang with his hand over his heart, his face a portrait of mock melancholy.

"Somebody *loves* you," Katy corrected quietly.

George with an exaggerated bow, stepped forward. "Who can he be? He is me!" Thigh-slapping laughter. Katy moved closer to the bar to watch George. All four men saw her in the mirror. She turned away, hiding her face in the dark side of the room.

"George, you dirty old singing son of a gun . . ." Louie walked up to him and cuffed him on the shoulder.

There was another rumble of thunder.

"You're gettin' real good with the cowboy talk," George replied.

Louie looked at Katy. "You just watch," he grinned. "Why howdy, little lady, welcome to winny-muck-a, nee-va-day, paradise of thee west."

"Heavy," said George.

"Hi," said Katy.

"Katy, this is Louie; Louie, this is Katy," George

said, "George, this is Katy; Louie, this is George." More laughter.

Katy reached for a chair, pulled it away from the table, and sat down. It was amazing, she thought. Louie and George looked enough alike to be brothers.

"You two should be on television," Katy said. "Like the Smothers Brothers, only cousins."

"When we were kids," Louie said, looking at Katy, "me and George lived in the same town. Our mothers thought it would be nice if we took tap-dancing lessons. I don't guess George has told you about our golden years on the stage."

"We danced at every Catholic dinner for three years. Started when we were six," George added.

"George moved," Louie explained. "Thereby ending a brilliant career."

"You guys are shittin'," one of the men at the bar said.

"You fucker, who would lie about a thing like that?" Louie shouted.

Katy pushed her pack under the chair. "You must have taken plenty of gas from your friends."

"What friends?" George asked.

"The life of a star is a lonely one," Louie said, leaning closer to Katy.

He smelled vaguely of garlic.

"The shit came down in sort of this order," Louie raised and lowered his eyebrows, Groucho Marx style. "Bring us a couple a beers, George."

He sat down next to Katy. George dumped his bag by the pinball machine and went behind the bar.

"My grandma was the boss. Mama mia, she was a tough old lady. The mafia could have used her. My aunt Millie teaches tap dancing and ballet, right? So Grandma says to my mom and to George's mom, you girls will help your sister get started. Everybody will take dancing lessons."

Katy smiled. No one in her family ever insisted that anyone do anything. She supposed they were more democratic. Actually, she thought, no one cared that much.

George brought three glasses of draft beer and put one in front of each of them. As he placed the last one on the table, he tipped it, spilling the foam. He reached for paper napkins from the container on the table and proceeded to mop while Louie went on with the story.

"So my mother, she says to me, 'You, Louie, will take tap dancing. The girls can take ballet.' 'No,' I say. 'Yes,' she says, and she looks up at the belt on the hook."

George seemed a little embarrassed and looked down at his glass of beer.

" 'You gonna dance, one way or another,' she said." Louie laughed.

Katy smiled.

"So George and I danced, oh boy, did we dance."

"The stars of the Rigatelli dancing school."

"What did the other kids think?" Katy asked.

Louie leaned back in his chair. "Not much for long." He reached over and punched George on the bicep. "There were two of us, and if any dummy said anything whatever about the dancing, George and me would wait behind a bush, or a tree, or a fence, and when that kid came ramblin' by, he got punched. Physical violence, they call it, and it worked damn fucking well."

Katy took a sip of the beer, then a long swallow.

"I left Rosa and Johnny's," George said to Louie. "Shit, they were making me damned nervous. That Rosa's crazy, I tell you."

"You're lucky Grandma's dead and gone, boy," Louie said. He looked at Katy. "So where you and George headed?"

"We're not exactly together," Katy said.

"It's a long story," George added.

Katy took another sip of beer. "You know," she said, "my grandmother wears purple and orange kaftans with white geese flying sideways. She says things like 'heavy' and 'up tight.' "

George and Louie looked at her quizzically.

"So how did you two meet?" Louie asked.

"She was riding with the guy that gave me a ride, after I split from Elko."

"It's funny," Katy said. "My grandmother looks like an old hippie, sandals and all."

"Our grandma looked like an old lady, black dress, white hair, belt in hand." Louie sighed. "A kindly white-haired old lady."

"Ha!" said George.

"Ha, ha," said Louie.

A young man with a freckled face came into the Pizza Place and sat down at the bar. He removed his cowboy hat and put it on the stool next to him. Greetings were exchanged and Louie got up to serve him.

Katy touched George's arm. "Hey," she whispered, "you seemed funny when we got out of that car. What was wrong?"

Then the Pizza Place filled with music. One of the young men stood at the jukebox.

Phoebe Snow sang "Let the Good Times Roll."

"Listen," George said, "they gave me the creeps with all that religious stuff. I had an uncle who talked like that."

Louie was back at the table.

"So you want to crash here for a while?" he looked at George, then Katy.

"Yes. Listen, you got any jobs open now?" George asked. "For a star chef?"

"Let me put it this way," Louie said, winking at Katy, "I got a guy who's not doing too good behind the bar while I spin my famous pizza in the kitch. If he's two minutes late tonight, something might be coming up."

Laughing and lifting of beer glasses, and Katy listened while they talked of old times, stunts, shenanigans.

"You should have seen what we did to the junior high principal," George said. "We always played our tricks late at night, by the way."

"We piled horse shit on newspaper, lit it on fire, rang his doorbell, and ran." Louie howled, throwing back his head.

"You should have seen him stomping away on that shit—in his house slippers." George laughed too.

"It must have been fun to grow up in a small town," Katy said.

"Who grew up?" Louie asked.

"Berkeley, well, it tends to be so stimulating there isn't time for fun," she said.

"What does that mean?" George asked.

"Oh, dancing lessons, gymnastics, Camp Fire Girls, swimming lessons, violin lessons, horseback-riding lessons, tennis lessons . . ."

"Tough life," said George.

"Sure, 'tis," Louie agreed.

"I was going to go to college," said Katy.

"Oh," said Louie and George at the same time.

Phoebe Snow sang on the jukebox, and Katy mouthed the familiar words.

George tapped the table with his fingers.

"Hey, well," said Louie, standing from the table. "Let's get your gear into the back."

"You want to stay, or do you want to go on to Berkeley right away?" George asked her.

"I'd like to stay for a day or so, if that's okay," she said. He didn't see the tears in her eyes.

"Is that all right?" George turned to Louie.

"Sure, no hassle," Louie answered, his face passive. "It ain't the Ritz . . ." Louie clapped his hands together and did a fast shuffle with his canvas-soled feet. "We never played the Ritz." He bowed.

George laughed, and the cousins slapped hands.

Katy giggled through her tears. "Thanks," she said. George helped her up, and Louie led the way to the back of the restaurant.

Louie's living quarters consisted of two rooms. The first contained a water bed covered with a madras spread, a lumpy couch, and a dresser with one drawer missing. Old vaudeville posters lined the wall.

"I wanted to have my tap shoes bronzed, but my mother threw them away," Louie said.

The other room had linoleum on the floor. The pattern was that of a flowered rug, and it looked antique in a yellow way. Four bulky overstuffed chairs sat in a row along one wall. From the arm of the red chair sprouted a long, trailing ivy plant. A pot was embedded in the upholstery, and the vine gave the impression that the chair was filled with earth and tangled roots. A mirror stretched across the wall opposite the chairs.

"This is really weird," Katy said.

"We don't have TV," Louie said, "so we watch ourselves."

"Hey, Louie, customer." A shout from the front.

Another Phoebe Snow song was blasting away on the jukebox.

"Throw your junk anywhere you want," Louie said, and with a dramatic salute to his image in the mirror, he went back to the bar.

"Thanks," Katy said to George. "You've been a really big help to me."

"Sure," George said, as he placed his bag on the floor next to some large flowered pillows.

"I just don't know what happened with Mr. Batinovich," she said. "What made him that mad." Katy stood by the chair with the ivy arm. "And those people we rode with!"

George turned to her, a peculiar look in his eyes.

"Listen," he said. "They just made me nervous, okay?" He looked away from her only to be confronted with his own image in the mirror, and her face reflecting at him from the other direction.

"I had an uncle once; he was kind of crazy. He used to get drunk and stumble through town holding a cross in front of him. You couldn't understand exactly what he was saying, he was so drunk."

George turned around to face Katy. The tap-dancing rhythm was gone.

"My grandma used to say something awful would happen to him."

"What did happen to him?" Katy asked, softly.

"He got murdered," George said. "Somebody gave him a ride out into the desert, cut off his arm, and left him there."

Katy sank down into one of the soft chairs. She looked at her hands. "Who did it?" she asked.

George frowned. "They don't know."

"How long ago did this happen?"

"Three years ago this month," George said. "Grandma said it was Uncle George's sins."

"George?" Katy asked. "His name was George?"

"I was named for him. Isn't that heavy?" George's face was rigid, his eyes dark and still. "It gives me the creeps."

Louie shuffled back into the room.

"What happened to the forehead?" he asked, moving to Katy and looking closely at the cut. "And the neck? Run into a vampire?"

"I hit the dashboard when Mr. Batinovich stopped," she answered.

"You two must have had a freak-out trip," Louie said. "Get set up and you can have the privilege of helping me in the wonderful world of Pizza tonight." He did another quick step. "Hey, boys and girls, why don't we put on a show?" He high-stepped from the room, tipping an imaginary hat.

George pulled off his tee shirt and went into the bathroom. He closed the door, and Katy was alone with her image in the mirror. She walked closer to examine the cut on her forehead. For the amount of bleeding, the abrasion was small. If she combed her hair right, she could cover it. And the mark on her neck was a tiny round scab. But her cheeks were hot, as if someone had slapped her.

She did not want George to be upset. She particularly did not want him to be angry with her. He had been so wonderful. His arms around her as they stood by the side of the road. George with his beautiful black hair. He really had rescued her, she thought.

She could hear the sound of the shower, water running steadily. She went to the window, pulled the flimsy net curtains aside and looked out. A row of dirty metal garbage cans lined the alley. A rickety flight of outside stairs ascended the two-story building across from her, and a sign on the door at the top read, NO ENTRY. The sun was out again. She looked over the buildings and houses to the low mountains. There was a brilliant rainbow forming over the foothills.

"George?" she called, but he could not hear her over the sound of the shower. "George, you should see. There's a great rainbow."

The water continued to run.

Katy lifted the window from the bottom, and the scent of rain-washed air rushed in at her.

She rubbed her arms. She needed a shower, too. She was covered with a gritty layer of dust.

And from the bar, she could hear yet another Phoebe Snow song.

> *"There was a man who loved so hard*
> *He was like a billboard grin*
> *He toasted life and beauty*
> *'Til his head began to spin*
> *He pressed his cheek*
> *On rainwashed streets*
> *And he wept into his gin*
> *Reincarnation*
> *And he came back as himself again."*

After she showered, while George and Louie talked more about their families, Katy went for a walk. It wasn't that the stories weren't interesting, weren't funny. But she could feel herself sulking. Her family was nice; it wasn't that. But George and Louie seemed to have had all these people around. Interesting people. Crazy people like Uncle George. Everyone in her family seemed so "occupied."

She turned onto the main street, and stood deciding which direction to walk. The business section was one building deep, and was composed of drugstores with old-fashioned fountain service, five-and-dime stores, and mercantiles. The buildings were generally old, not more than two stories high, and occasionally a merchant had added a new front, but the backs of the buildings were, for the most part, brick or stucco in need of paint. The casinos were the brightly decorated buildings with signs with replaceable letters announcing the special for the day, the week, or the summer. The people on the street, tourists, travelers, and shoppers, walked quickly, with places to go. Perhaps they scurried in order to avoid another shower, another clap of thunder. She smiled at the wooden Indian in front of the Star Broiler.

Families. Her brothers, Ross and Kenneth, would go on to some good college. It wasn't that she didn't like them. A few years ago, they had teased and tormented her in an affectionate way. They were serious now. Nobody in her family clowned around the way George and Louie did. What would they say when they found out she was pregnant? In Berkeley, children learned about things like that in the fourth grade. They would hardly be shocked. And her parents? An embarrassment, probably. What about all that sex education, they would ask. Why didn't it work? Of course her father would arrange an abortion, but she wouldn't agree. She would insist on keeping the child. She was an old-fashioned girl, and they would have to *deal* with that.

She walked down to the end of the block and crossed the street. She stepped around the puddles of rainwater, and dodged a boy on a bike. She imagined Sam's family was more like George and Louie's. A family where, when one member was gone, it made a difference.

And suddenly, she found herself standing in front

of Sam's station wagon. The license plate holder. Albany. She put her hand on the fender, amazed at the whiteness, the glare of it all. Drops of water were drying on the windshield. He must be in the casino, she thought. In the cafe, the bar.

She could leave him a note. Yes. That was the thing to do. A note saying she was sorry, really sorry. A note saying she was all right. She was certain he was worried because he was that kind of person.

She looked about frantically for a place that she might get a piece of paper and a pencil. She could write it out and put it under the windshield wiper. He would see it for sure. She would tell him that she was down the street, around the corner at the Pizza Place. I am all right, she would say, and I am sorry for anything I said that upset you. Thank you for the ride.

Paper and pencil. The cafe. A waitress would have both. She pushed through the doors of Kristo's, and stood in the carpeted lobby searching for the right direction. A woman in a short black skirt and a red off-the-shoulder blouse walked by carrying an empty tray.

"Could I borrow a piece of paper and a pencil to write a note?" Katy pleaded. "Just for a second."

The waitress looked annoyed for a moment, then smiled. She took an extra pencil from the pocket of her skirt, and pulled a blank check from her pad.

"A love note?" she asked softly.

"Not exactly," Katy smiled. "More like an apology."

"That's pretty much the same thing," Shirl said. "Just leave the pencil at the cashier's." She looked for a moment as if she might touch Katy in some gesture of sympathy, or longing, but she did not.

The note completed, Katy returned the pencil, and went outside. His station wagon was still there, and she lifted the windshield wiper and placed the note underneath. Perhaps when he read it, he would come to the Pizza Place and they could talk. She did not see Shirl, who had paused in front of the casino door to watch.

Katy ran back down the street, skipping around the puddles, happy in the clean-smelling, crystal-clear air of resolution. She would not mention the note to George; he wouldn't understand.

A policeman checked the chalk mark on the right rear tire of the station wagon. He shook his head, and noted the license plate number on the ticket. Overtime in a twenty-four minute zone. When he lifted the windshield wiper to place the ticket there, a slight gust of wind blew a small piece of paper into the gutter. He watched the water swallow the paper and carry it away. He shrugged his shoulders and hoped it wasn't important. It was too late to do anything about it now.

Kristo had called the manager of the nicest motel in Winnemucca and arranged a room for Sam. It was as simple as that for Kristo, and Sam was impressed.

When he stood in front of the station wagon, staring at the ticket, he merely shook his head and muttered, "When things go wrong . . ."

And when he stood in the middle of the room, his suitcase beside him, he smiled and remembered that it was not always so. Not always did he stay in good motels. Early on the route, well, the places weren't exactly fleabags, but the motels and hotels did not have what one could call "class."

When was it, Sam wondered as he picked up the bag and placed it on the suitcase rack, that he had made the transition from motels that made him long for the comfort of home to motels that made his own living room look shabby?

"You know summer. All these travelers," Kristo had nodded at him. "The motels fill up fast. The best ones first. Isn't that the way of things now? But what the hell, I've done some favors for Mitchell in my day. The last one—catered a party for some movie crew at his place. Had maybe ten minutes notice. Oh, there's a story in that day, my friend."

Sam opened the suitcase. He hoped he had a clean shirt left. If he hung his suit in the bathroom while he showered it would look better. He wondered if one of the movie stars had stayed in this very room. Movie stars in Winnemucca. Wouldn't Julianna get a kick out of that. Daddy slept in a room where Clint Eastwood slept, or maybe even John Wayne. Someone famous. In the bottom of the bag was a light blue shirt, folded neatly. Luck. A blue shirt for the birthday boy.

He turned and caught his reflection in the dresser mirror. His beard was beginning to shadow his chin. He rubbed the stubble with one hand. He looked pale, a little gray, like the rain-showered sky. He narrowed his eyes. He was a dark man, shadowed and rumpled in a room with gold shag carpet and white furniture. Paintings on the walls and hanging lamps on each side of the bed. The sunlight made the white drapes luminous. He could hear the noise from the swimming pool. Splashes, giggles, children playing in the water. Squeals.

The image of the little girl in the sunsuit passed quickly through his mind and became Julianna in another time. Sam wished he had a bathing suit. Made a mental note to take one on trips from now on. He would stay at places with pools. He could use the exercise.

But Shirl had looked at him, sidelong. She was a flirt. Was it part of her job? Maybe it was a birthday gift Kristo had asked her to give him.

He walked to the window, pulled the drapes, and looked out across the lawn to the swimming pool. A little boy in a yellow suit stood shivering on the end of the board. Someone in the water wanted him to jump. Arms were held up, the fingers coaxed. The boy stood, his knees together, the water running down his face from his hair. He bent over enough to look into the face that belonged to the waiting arms.

"Come on," a voice called. "Come on now, jump."

Sam turned away. He could not bear to watch the trembling boy standing on the end of the board, his fear nailed and dripping about for all to see.

Sam muttered, "God dammit, jump" to himself. "Sooner or later, we all have to jump."

He heard the pulsing wail of an ambulance rushing along the street and wondered before he could stop himself if it was anyone he knew. Habit from growing up in a small town. Reflex fear. There you would know who it was. Not here.

At five o'clock he would call Thelma. Could he tell her about Katy and George? Could he say to her, hell, this kid asked me for a ride, and I didn't have the good sense to tell her no, and then she was in the car and all I could think about was Julianna and all I could think was that Julianna was dead and this girl, this Katy, was alive. Then I picked up a boy as if it wasn't bad enough to pick up the girl. Hell, these damned kids, they keep at you. I couldn't take it anymore, so I stopped the car and asked them to get out. Could he tell Thelma that?

Could he explain to anyone why he could not bear to look at either one of those kids. All he could think of was one amputated life, his Julianna's, her womanhood severed and gone.

He opened his shaving kit, and took out the razor and cream. It would be nice to be able to use an electric razor, he thought, but he couldn't get a close enough shave. It's the Yugoslav whiskers, tough black stubs.

Tough like your father, tough, black-eyed bastard. Beard persists, like his stare.

Thelma would chastise him for picking up a hitchhiker. She would talk about danger, robbery, beatings, maimings, murder. She would make him feel like a coward. He would remind her of the gun. She would remind him not to shoot himself accidentally, then he would feel like a fool, too.

No. He would call her and tell her that he loved her, that he hoped she was getting along, and that he would be home tomorrow night. She would tell him Happy Birthday, Sam; we'll have a party, yes a party, when you get here. And he would tell her about the fancy room Kristo had arranged and about the dinner they would have later. He wouldn't mention the belly dancer.

There wasn't anyone he could tell about Katy. He wondered how long it would take to forget the look on her face, and the blood that ran into her eye.

He turned on the television set and Walter Cronkite came into focus. He looked stern and scolding as he talked about a kidnapping. Sam shook his head. The world was filled with crazy people, it was true. He could not in honesty say, when Thelma worried, that the world was a safe place.

He left the television on while he shaved. He did not listen carefully to the news, only to the sound of another voice. They gave the baseball scores and the Dow-Jones average. The President was away at his weekend retreat.

Then he showered, and all the words were gone, and he was enveloped in hot water and steam. He thought he might be washing all of the remnants of the day away in the whirlpool that formed at his feet and circled into the drain. He soaped his chest and arms, the dark hair curling in patterns, wiry beneath his fingers. He felt the sharp shooting water on his face, massaging, relaxing, cleaning away the dust of the highway, the blood.

But he did not have blood on *his* face. He shook his

head, closed his eyes, and let the water pound his body. He wondered if he could go to sleep in the shower. He opened his eyes. The thought of sleep. Nights lying in bed. That was when the ghosts came. How many nights had he been unable to sleep with the feel of Julianna's hand in an unrelenting grip so real his hand would begin to tingle. Her poor dead form caught and pinned in his mind. Eyes open, eyes closed; he saw it and his heart ached. And although he and Thelma had created Julianna in that very bed, he could not reach for her. He did not know what she saw when she looked at her dead child. She never told him.

And he had never asked. Sam turned the water off abruptly. It might be easier if they talked about things. If they sat around some night and talked about their daughter and what it felt like to lose her.

He dried his body with the soft white towels of the motel. He used two towels. He rubbed his skin, fluffing the hair on his chest. He looked at the television screen. Andy Griffith and his son, Opie, were walking along to the music that introduced the show. Going fishing. Tom Sawyer, barefoot in the dust. Sam smiled. A happy kid walking along with his pa. Not a trembling boy on the end of a diving board.

He wrapped a towel around his waist and sat down at the table near the window. He read the instructions for placing a long distance call that were printed on the card attached to the telephone. Anxious for the first time in a while to hear the sound of Thelma's voice, he picked up the receiver.

He let the telephone ring so long that finally the operator came on the line and said, "That party is not at home; would you like to replace the call later?"

He mumbled, not prepared to speak to the operator, only prepared to speak to Thelma. Dinner time, she was always home. His birthday, she knew he would call. Where was she? He thought he should be worried, but he could feel only irritation.

Wasn't anyone where they were supposed to be today?

He looked at the telephone, picked up the receiver, and replaced the call. He said each number slowly, carefully, so the operator would not make a mistake.

Again, there was no answer. Thelma was simply not at home. Hell, she could be at the grocery store, next door with the neighbors, at some class—any number of places. It was just that, usually, she was home.

He could not remember a time when she had not been there when he called. Always the same time. He looked at his watch. Five-ten.

He swallowed and noticed that the aftertaste of the champagne was not so sweet. He went into the bathroom to brush his teeth. He would then be a totally clean man.

Where was she?

He could try again, just before he went back to Kristo's place at six. He pulled back the drapes and stared out at the pool. Several women reclined on the lounges, skin greased and shiny in the late afternoon sun.

It wouldn't be dark until after nine in Winnemucca.

He let the drape fall back into place. He took off the towel and lay down naked on the bed to watch the television. He watched without interest. Aunt Bea was taking flying lessons. An old lady learning to fly a plane. Laughter in the background of the show. Laughter and splashes from the swimming pool just outside his window. Sam looked at his body. He touched the hair around his groin. Aunt Bea was getting her pilot's license and everyone was saying that they knew all along she could do it. She was laughing, smiling, blushing. Pleased as punch, she said.

Sam confused arousal with a spasm of pain. He

thought about Shirl and her blouse that could be so easily pulled down, about Katy and her body against his as he held her, and he could not stop the desire. He rolled onto his stomach and closed his eyes. Happy Birthday, Sam Batinovich, happy birthday to you.

He awoke with the distinct feeling that something was wrong. The dreams, however brief, had escaped without memory, leaving only the vague feeling of displeasure, and he glanced at his watch, sat up quickly, aware that he would be late. He was chilled. The air conditioning suddenly too cool for his body. On the television screen, he saw Gilligan running through the jungle pursued by a gorilla. What was it that made children love "Gilligan's Island"? A bunch of nincompoops stranded. Sam walked to the set and changed the channel. The evening news bounced at him, a map of the Middle East to the right of Harry Reasoner's face.

Sam dressed quickly. The suit looked pretty good. He picked those socks that he had worn longest ago. Kristo always wore a tie. Sam reached into his suitcase for the one he carried, but rarely wore. He guessed Julianna had given it to him for Christmas or Father's Day. Some such occasion. He could not remember. The tie was dark blue with light blue stars, and little gold moons. An india print fabric of some kind.

Once, he'd had a tie with a naked lady painted on the wide part. It had come with a battery to be carried in his pocket. When he pushed the button, the lady's nipples lit up. He could flash them, wink them at people. The boys on the bowling team gave him the tie as a present. Highest average. Years ago. They insisted he put it on. It embarrassed him to think about it even now. But hell, was that any worse than the woman on the Johnny Carson show? The one with the winking sequin eyes plastered right on top of her breasts.

The temperature was still close to ninety as Sam walked down the sidewalk toward Kristo's place. The air was hot and dry after the slightly damp coolness of his room. He felt his skin begin to tighten on his face. He walked casually with one hand in his pocket, his fingers around the key to his room.

A family—mother, father, little boy, and three little girls stood in the middle of the sidewalk. They wore summer clothes and held white soft-ice-cream cones in their hands. All except one. The smallest girl was crying, and the family stood in a circle looking at the smashed and rapidly melting cone that lay on the sidewalk.

Sam smiled. *I scream, you scream, we all scream for ice cream.*

"Daddy will get you another one," the woman said.

"Janie dropped her ice cream, Janie dropped her ice cream," the little boy sang.

Janie wailed and hit her brother with a sticky hand.

Sam stepped into the gutter to walk around the family. He almost laughed. He felt good, all dressed up, some-place to go. Hell, he had forgotten in his rush to call Thelma. He could call from Kristo's office. Sure, call collect. He was already late.

Kristo was still sitting at his desk when Sam knocked.

"Hey, you get all settled down? Ready for a big night on the town?" Kristo's face wrinkled into a handsome smile. "Hey, for an old man, you look pretty sharp. Don't you think so, Shirl?"

Sam had not noticed the woman who sat in a chair in the corner of the room. He felt his face flush with em-barrassment. Caught doing something he shouldn't.

Shirl put her cigarette to her lips, nodded and smiled, inhaled, and said, "You're a good-looking man, Sam." She raised a glass that contained what looked like whiskey over ice. "Happy Birthday."

Sam thought it did not seem appropriate to call Thelma right at that moment. He wondered, as he straightened his tie, what exactly was the connection between Kristo and Shirl.

"I think I better have a drink," Sam said.

"Shirl will mix you one while I clean up a little," Kristo said, rising from behind the desk. He winked at Sam as he opened the door to the bathroom.

"We've got Scotch and bourbon up here," Shirl said as she stood. "If you want something else, I can order it brought up from the bar."

She no longer wore the red off-the-shoulder blouse, the uniform of a cocktail waitress. She was dressed in a short clinging jersey dress with a low round neck and long sleeves. She looked like somebody's girl friend.

"I'll have bourbon and water," Sam said. He stared at her legs and the high white heels she wore as she stood mixing the drink.

"I'm off tonight, so Kristo thought I should join your party." She turned and handed him the drink. "Is that all right with you, Sam?"

She looked him straight in the eye as she asked, and Sam felt compelled to return the directness of her gaze.

"More the merrier, they say," he smiled, and he could feel his face quiver slightly. The strain, the smile. He took a deep drink of the bourbon, looking for peace. From the bathroom came the sound of Kristo's electric razor. Sam looked with relief toward the door.

"Worked here long?" he asked.

"Less than a year," Shirl replied, handing her lighter to Sam, and placing a cigarette between her lips. She came close to him, waiting. His hands felt gigantic; he thought he might drop the lighter. She stood even closer, and as he managed to flick the lighter into flame, he could see the tops of her breasts and smell a perfume.

She inhaled and stood back from him. "I used to be a dealer in Reno. Got tired of it."

Sam nodded, as if he understood what she meant.

"Here, I have more responsibility, more variety," she added.

Sam took a deep breath. The sense of the motel room, lying on the bed, his naked body, dampness, the air conditioner kept returning to him. He tried to fix his memory on the splattered ice cream cone on the street. On the shivering boy at the end of the diving board.

"Kristo is a good man to work for," she said and sat back down in the chair. Sam leaned against the desk and faced her. "I think I'll stay for a while, anyway." She smiled.

Sam had difficulty seeing the woman all at once. He picked out parts of her. Her face was pretty enough, he supposed. She wore bright red lipstick and he thought most women didn't do that anymore. It left marks on her cigarettes. Still, it looked nice on her.

He really should call Thelma. There must be a way. Why didn't he just ask Shirl if he could use the phone? It was damned clear that if Shirl was anybody's business, she was Kristo's, so what difference would it make if he called his wife in front of her?

"How long are you planning to stay in town?" she asked.

"Oh, I guess I'll leave tomorrow. Should get on to Reno. Check on some customers there." Sam said the words slowly. He looked once again toward the door. The razor was silent now. What was Kristo doing?

"Come through here often?" Shirl asked. She swung

one crossed leg slightly as she talked. She was relaxed. She seemed to know what she was supposed to do, to say, Sam thought.

"Well, I've been off schedule some lately. Usually I hit Oregon, Idaho, western states, you know, mostly take orders, look for new accounts. I like the travel."

Christ, he didn't know why he said that. Hell, he didn't like the travel.

"Hey, Kristo," he called, "what's holding you up?" He looked back to Shirl and laughed. "He always so slow?"

"He's careful," Shirl said. "A very careful man."

Sam did not know how long he was going to be able to keep this chitchat going. She seemed to understand something he did not. She continued to draw on her cigarette. She rarely took her eyes off Sam. He felt like pacing. He turned toward the window. He looked out onto the street. The winking blinking stars of the Star Broiler and Casino were still there. He looked down at the blue stars and gold moons on his tie.

"That was some storm we had today, wasn't it?" he said.

"Yes," Kristo answered, as he opened the door from the bathroom and emerged. "Bringing in the birthday with a thunder and a bang, so to say," he laughed. "And besides, it is Thor's day. Thor with his hammer, his thunder, his strength. Thursday. See?"

The tightness in Sam's throat released as he nodded at Kristo.

"We'll start with a drink at my table in the bar, maybe you want to shoot some craps, eh, Sam? Give me a little of your money before dinner?"

Sam smiled as Shirl came toward him.

"Come on, you old devils," she said as she took Sam's arm. "This party is about to begin."

They sat in the elevated corner booth in the dark lounge. The waitress took their orders, and Sam excused himself.

The telephone rang and rang. There was no answer. It was seven o'clock on his birthday and Thelma was not home. When he walked back to the booth, he sat down next to Shirl. He could feel her leg next to his, and she was warm. Kristo once again proposed a toast, and Shirl leaned closer to Sam.

She was indeed warm in the midst of the air-conditioned breeze.

Sam remembered the ice cream on the street, the key in his pocket, the white drapes of his room. He heard the solitary ringing of the telephone, and he wondered where the hell his wife was.

He asked Shirl for a cigarette. One wouldn't hurt. And he was grateful when she lit it for him so he could hide his shaking hands.

At ten minutes to five, twenty-three Jehovah's Witnesses came through the door of the Pizza Place, pushed three tables together, and sat down.

"We're on our way to Canada for a conference," a short bald man said to Katy as she handed him the menu. "We're traveling in a caravan."

"What kind of conference?" Katy asked as she put a menu before a young woman in a striped cotton dress.

"The Jehovah's Witnesses of the world," the large woman at the head of the table said in a loud voice.

"Do you have a pizza with just plain yellow cheese?" a little boy asked.

"I'll check," Katy said.

"This is our whole group, sitting right here," the large woman said proudly. She waved one fleshy arm magnanimously over the flock. "We are all from the town of Auburn, California."

Katy took glasses of iced water from the stand in the corner and placed them around. George came over with extra silverware and napkins. He smiled at her as he passed by.

She had not told George about the note, and the rainbow had disappeared by the time she got back. All she could do was point to where the band of color had been and tell George about it. And now, everytime someone came through the door, Katy expected it to be Sam. Certainly he would let her say she was sorry. All the time she talked to George, she watched the door. George had been to college for a year in Reno. He told her more about his family, but he did not mention his uncle again.

And Louie had said, "You will waita the tables, Katrina, and dona forgetta the Italiano. Sells more pizza."

Katy laughed, but was reminded of Sam's joke.

"Mama mia," she replied, "or words to that effect."

Laughter. Louie and George were always dancing, cutting up, kidding around. Handsome George. Nice George.

In the kitchen, she asked Louie, "Do you have a pizza for a little boy? He wants plain yellow cheese."

"Grab the food coloring, Fatso," Louie called to the cook.

"Seriously, a little boy asked."

"We can make up a little one. What the hell. There is no artistry left in the world. Today yellow cheese, tomorrow Velveeta, the day after that . . . God, what could be worse than Velveeta." Louie shrugged.

Back in the dining room, Katy whispered to the boy that he could have his yellow cheese pizza.

The Jehovah's Witnesses did not drink beer. George served them milk and Seven-Up. Katy took their orders.

"Mushroom and sausage, two green salads with Thousand Island dressing."

Carefully, she printed the words on the yellow pad. Four men in cowboy garb—denim and white hats, plaid shirts—came through the door, young and wiry, energetic and loud against the family-style din created by the Witnesses.

"You son-of-a-bitch, the next time you get in my way"
—one tanned young man playfully pushed another one—
"I'll run over both them pointed toe feet 'a yours with
a goddamned herd of buffalo."

The Witnesses, to a person, looked alarmed. To a
person, they sat with hands folded on the table as if
waiting to pray.

"Watch your language, please," Katy said as she
passed by the cowboys. "There are kids at that table
over there."

"Sssh," came the reply from one cowboy as he shook
his finger at the other. "You fuckers better watch your
fucking tongues."

Katy went through the door into the kitchen, shaking
her head in disgust. Louie shrugged and turned away.
The slicer was creating a mound of thin salami. Fatso
spun and flipped the crust, and they were too busy to
worry about twenty-three Jehovah's Witnesses objecting
to foul language.

When she went back into the room, several other
people had entered the restaurant. George placed glasses
of iced water in front of them. She picked up the plastic
menus and distributed them.

"Thank you, miss, yes, indeed. Thirsty. Hot out on that
desert." A couple, a man and a woman with matching
blue checkered shirts. The woman wore an obvious blond
wig. They looked to be mid-forty.

"We're newlyweds," the man grinned and winked.

"Congratulations," said Katy. "Wow."

The cowboys were still raucous at the bar, but now
two tables of customers separated them from the Witnesses. Every time the door opened, the Witnesses were
struck by the shaft of daylight while the cowboys basked
in the artificial glitter of the bar and the mirror. Blue

denim, white hats, bronze faces, and steel words, brown shiny bottles of beer, and laughter. One cowboy's teeth glittered gold when he smiled, dazzled when he laughed.

The Witnesses ate quietly, solemnly separated from the melee by the newlyweds and a family of four.

"My pizza was the very best," the little boy said. "Mine had yellow cheese."

Katy almost patted him on the head. She moved around the table with the white plastic pitcher of water, refilling glass after glass, splashing minimally.

As Katy returned the pitcher to a stand, George said in his best Humphrey Bogart voice, "Listen, sweetheart, let's get out of this place." He touched her lightly on her bare shoulder.

Katy laughed. "I think this is fun," she said.

"Mama mia," George replied, and went into the kitchen.

"You were very nice," the large woman said. "We'd like you to have some of our literature." She handed Katy a stack of pamphlets. The flesh swung under the woman's arms like flat sacks.

Then the Witnesses in unison stood, as if there existed a signal for rising from the table. Chairs were moved back, and they were ready to leave.

Katy smiled and said good-bye to them as they left.

The cowboys had ordered a pizza. It was ready, and she asked if they wanted to move to a table. They could not even seem to walk that far without jostling one another, with shoving, laughing, swearing.

And then, as she was carrying the pizza, a "Louie Deluxe" with everything but anchovies, the door opened and a young man entered. Katy was stunned. He was silhouetted in the doorway; she was certain it was Kurt. He must be looking for her. She had not even really dared to think it possible, but what other reason would he have for being here? Should she run to him and throw her arms around his neck? Or perhaps she should be angry at first, make him plead with her for forgiveness. Trembling, she started toward him.

Then it happened. She caught the toe of her sandal on a chair leg and stumbled forward. She struggled to hold the pizza in front of her, to keep the tray level. She lurched, then drew back, then fell again. One hand left the tray and smashed flat-palmed into the middle of one cowboy's back. As he turned, the pizza flew from the tray, slapped feebly at his face, and draped about his shoulder.

The cowboy screamed, a piercing "wahoo." The melted cheese, hot and bubbling, had attached to his neck and hardened. He pulled at the threads, the cheese sticking to his fingers. He stood, knocking his chair over, and Katy moved back away.

"When the moon hits your eye like a big pizza pie," sang Louie from behind the bar, "that's *amore*."

"I'm sorry, oh God, I'm sorry," Katy said. She did not move. The pizza was a crumpled mass on the floor. The cowboy, in a rage, put his boot into the middle of it.

"Goddamned son-of-a-bitch, Christ almighty . . ."

And the young blond man who Katy thought was Kurt Edwards stepped into the light, and there was not even that much resemblance. Tears came to Katy's eyes. Laughter filled the room, and the young blond man laughed the loudest of all. The Witnesses were gone, but the people at other tables turned to see.

"Oh my," said the newlywed woman.

"Golly," said the man.

"It's all right," Louie said.

"It's all right," George mimicked.

"Settle down, now Jas, it was an accident," Louie said to the cowboy who doubled his fist and threatened him.

"Order another Louie Deluxe," George called to the kitchen.

Katy held the metal tray. She knelt to the floor and began to scoop the mangled pizza onto the plate. Kurt was never coming after her—never. The cheese burned her fingers; tears rolled down her cheeks. She kept her head down. If only Sam would come through the door and tell her he would take her home.

"Bring four beers over here," Louie commanded. "Now listen, fellows, wasn't that a great show? And would you believe, this is Katy's very first night on the stage. And to have scored a direct hit. Quite an accomplishment."

He was laughing, and Katy began to laugh, too. Tears ran into her mouth, but she giggled, holding the tray with the unrecognizable pizza.

"What's going down?" a girl asked, and Katy turned to see a young woman in a checkered pinafore standing behind her. Her hair was shiny clean blond, and her skin was the color of sesame seeds. She put her hands on her hips.

"Dinah, this is Katy," Louie gestured. "New waitress, extraordinaire."

"Hi," Dinah said. "You don't look like much of a threat to my job," she added.

"Right," Katy said. "I'm certainly no threat."

As she stood to go back into the kitchen with the corpse of the pizza, a sharp pain kicked at her side. She touched her stomach gently, straightened, took a deep breath.

"Hello, sweetheart," one of the cowboys said to Dinah.

"Hello, Cale," she replied.

"You missed the show," Cale said, "you should have

seen the look on Jas's face when that pizza cracked him in the back." He hit Jas on the shoulder. "The dumb fucker."

"There are ladies present," said the newlywed man. His bride smiled at him.

"And children," said the father member of the family of four.

There was more laughter, clinking of beer mugs, all in the bright stained glass light of the bar.

"Don't give her a bad time," Katy heard Dinah say as she opened the kitchen door.

"Listen, I got cheese stuck to my neck that ain't never coming off," Jas said.

In the kitchen, Katy leaned against the counter and probed at the pain in her side. She looked at Fatso who was putting a pizza into the oven. His apron was tied tightly above his waist making a sausage roll at his middle. He turned back to the pizza makings, glanced at her, winked, and went to work.

Dinah came into the kitchen. She was a pretty girl, a country girl. Short hair, eyes that seemed too open. She was taller than Katy, and she looked older.

"The first day I worked here," Dinah said, "I dropped a whole tray of salads. Lettuce and pickled beets every-where. Louie still teases me." She turned to the small mirror on the wall by the door and touched her hair. "I'm glad to have some help."

Katy stretched. The pain was almost gone. She must have strained a muscle when she tripped.

"Thanks a lot," she said to Dinah. "Everyone's been nice to me." She stared at Dinah as the girl tied an apron over the pinafore.

"You look really familiar," Katy said. "Have you ever worked in Colorado?"

" 'Fraid not," Dinah smiled at her. "I'm Winnemucca born, and Winnemucca bred, and I guess I'll live in Winnemucca until I'm dead. How's that for a clever answer, compliments of Louie." She narrowed her eyes, then smiled brightly. Katy was hypnotized, staring at her.

"Maybe we met in another life. Reincarnation, you know. Do you like Phoebe Snow?" Dinah asked.

Fatso was chopping green peppers with a cleaver. A bell rang on the oven and he called to Katy. "Another Louie Deluxe coming up. Let's give it one more try, Sunshine."

"Yes," she said quickly to Dinah. "Yes, I like Phoebe Snow." She paused. "I know," she said, "you look like this little girl I met. I mean, like she'll look when she grows up."

"Oh?" said Dinah.

"Pizza," Fatso repeated.

"I promise I won't drop it," Katy said to him as she took it.

Dinah touched Katy's arm as she approached the door. "Listen," she said, "after we close up we can sit around and talk, okay? Louie and I usually have a couple of drinks."

When Katy walked into the dining room and put the pizza on the table in front of the blue-shirted cowboy, she received a round of applause. With a stiff smile, she bowed. The show must go on. But the little girl's face haunted her.

I'll be a sunbeam for Jesus, I'll be a sunbeam for Him.

The room was a theatre, the lights brilliant and jeweled. The Witnesses were gone. An empty table for twenty-three stood along the dark side of the room.

A man in walking shorts and a flowered shirt came

into the restaurant with a woman whose hair was in curlers. She carried a big straw purse with seashells and flowers attached to the sides. They sat on the side of the departed Witnesses, and George handed them menus.

"This here all right?" the man drawled to the woman, "This here table?"

She shrugged.

Dinah walked over to the couple and stood smiling pleasantly down at them, pad and pencil in hand while they scanned the menu. The woman asked a question. Dinah smiled and shook her head. George set glasses of water in front of them. The light flickered as the ice danced in the amber glasses.

"Hey," said one of the cowboys. "Hey, you—Kate. Isn't that your name?"

Katy turned to stare at him, her eyes unable to focus enough to see him clearly.

"Hey, why don't you and me have a drink later? I can show you my horse." He winked and the other cowboys roared with laughter.

"He can give you some ride, sweetheart," another cowboy said. "Just give him a little heel in the side and whoopee . . ."

The one named Cale laughed, his mouth full of beer, spraying the others. Katy looked, horrified, the lights and sounds closing in around her. Dinah, cool and clear in red and white, George wiping off the bar with a damp towel, people eating pizza, stringing the cheese, smiling. The pain in her side hit her with one more resounding knock.

"How 'bout it, honey, how about a midnight ride?"

Katy put her hand to the pain.

"Fuck off," she said, looking directly at the cowboy. She turned and walked to the comforting glitter of the long polished bar where George cleaned the counter with large circular strokes.

She guessed Sam wasn't going to come. She supposed she could call him when she got home to Berkeley. Then she imagined a woman answering the telephone and she knew she would not be able to call.

"Miss?" called the man with the southern drawl. "You got any Alka-Seltzer for the missus here?"

Katy looked to George.

"Sure," he said, tossing a packet to Katy. He drew a glass of water.

"We're from Florida," the man said as Katy handed the Alka-Seltzer to his wife. "And the West here has upset her stomach."

The woman eyed him with contempt as she dropped the powder into the water.

The warmth of Shirl's body next to his increased in direct proportion to the number of highballs Sam consumed. His hand, under the table, caressed her knee, sliding easily on her nylon stockings, and he looked down into her face and was able to smile without feeling lines stiffening around his mouth.

Kristo watched them with the joyful air of a satisfied madam, wiping his mouth with his napkin, leaning back in the booth, patting his stomach, content.

"So, pretty soon, the show starts, Sam. We'll see how Winnemucca takes to a belly dancer, hey?" Kristo winked.

Shirl put a cigarette to her lips, and Sam reached for the matches. She held his hand to steady the flame, and looked at his face.

Sam knew what was happening. He knew it was a set-up thing, but he didn't care. One takes a birthday gift where one finds it. He shouldn't throw away something so useful as this woman who sat beside him. Every time she touched him, her arm through his, her breast gently brushing his bicep, she startled and pleased him. Warm in the stomach, nervousness fleeing, and he did not think of Julianna, about death, or the cut on Katy's head. Setup or not, Shirl seemed to like him, wanted to touch him, wanted him to touch her back. She leaned her leg against his. She didn't pull back, fidget endlessly.

"So you grew up in Montana," she said to Sam. "We're country folk, you and me."

"Shirl's from Twin Falls, Idaho. She's come a long way . . . don't you think, Sam?" Kristo wasn't missing anything. He could see how Sam was feeling; Sam knew it.

"I go through Twin on my route. Have for years." He smiled at her. "You see that crazy Evel Knievel try to jump that canyon? You see that, Kristo? You ever seen that canyon?"

"I was hoping he'd land right smack in the bottom," she said quietly.

"I've seen that canyon," Kristo said.

"Strangest damned thing," Sam lifted his drink and looked out at the empty dance floor. "That canyon, flat as hell on both sides, then it's just like the earth split —like God made a trap. You can drive or walk, hell, right out to the edge, never see it coming. Must be like when they thought the world was flat. Fall off the edge. Damnedest thing."

Shirl touched Sam's hand. "Funny you should put it that way. When I was growing up there I had nightmares about falling into the canyon. Dreams just like that." She looked at his face, and she seemed younger, as if the memory had transported her physically into the past.

"I was afraid to go anywhere in the dark for fear I'd drop off the edge. Just like you said, I wouldn't see it coming."

"We all have our terrible dreams," Kristo said. "Our night fears."

"But that canyon was really there. It wasn't just a dream, see, that's the difference." Shirl shivered. Sam felt the vibration. "If you turned down the wrong street when you were riding your bike. It could happen any time. It could swallow you."

She stopped. "Hey—this is spooky. I'd like another drink." She looked about for the waitress, leaning forward over the table. Sam put his arm around her shoulders and when she looked at him in surprise, he bent and kissed her lightly on the cheek.

"We shouldn't talk about nightmares. Makes them return, makes us remember." The alcohol had changed the sound of his voice, changed the look in his eyes. He could feel it himself, and he watched, detached from his own body, barely recognizing the man who sat cuddling with the woman in the booth under the bemused patronage of Kristo. The vision was startlingly clear, like looking in a mirror, but he looked and there was no mirror.

The restaurant was crowded now. The customers were finishing their dinners, just as Sam and Shirl and Kristo had done before. Sam, if he had been asked, would not have remembered what he had just eaten. But then, who would ask, who would know how his mind was being consumed by the simple warmth of the woman next to him.

He began to see the necessity to have her, and he saw each detail of the motel room, white furniture, the bed, the telephone on the table. The ringing, ringing, ringing at his home, and Thelma was not there. He placed in his mind the image of Thelma sitting on the neighbor's patio, a glass of iced tea in her hand. She would be home later. He removed from his mind the vision of her lying on the bathroom floor. He cleaned up the blood, sopping it with a sponge. He did not know what someone would look like if they slashed their wrists. He supposed there would be blood everywhere. That would be it. Splattered on the tile, washing down the tub in crimson rivers. No. Thelma was not the type to do that. She worked at things carefully, steadily. She did not make sudden moves. He was the one who was apt to plunge. No. Thelma was sitting on the chaise longue, swirling the ice in the tall glass. But she was sad, and dammit he was glad he wasn't there. One red river running down the porcelain tub, then gone.

Kristo left the table to greet the Macedonian band. Sam leaned over Shirl and kissed her on the mouth. First softly, carefully, then he pushed at her, wanting her to know what he needed.

"Come back to my room with me," he whispered into her hair. Her hand was on his cheek. He could feel the fingers, slender, long-nailed, moving across his neck to his throat.

"Now?" she said, and he thought he could feel her smiling at his impatience.

"Now."

"What will Kristo think?" she caressed the back of his neck, making him want to pull her dress away from her breasts right there in the club.

"He'll think it's a nice way to spend my birthday." Sam listened to his own words in disbelief. And while he could feel his arms around her, feel her hand on the back of his neck, the mirror sensation remained, frightening him.

"Should I get a bottle from Kristo? Some bourbon?" She pulled away from him and straightened her hair.

"Yes," he said. He could feel the breath expanding in his lungs, feel the muscles of his arms tightening.

"It's pretty early," she said, smiling. She wasn't the little girl who worried about walking off the edge of the world. "We'll miss the belly dancer."

He took her hand and without looking at her whispered, "Please."

While she went to get the bottle and to tell Kristo,

Sam stood in the men's room and stared at his face in the mirror. He leaned against the washbasin and examined the man. He wavered slightly. More booze than he thought. The man looked younger than he remembered. More handsome. Yes, handsome. He washed his hands still checking the reflection. Strange. He was surprised when the image moved. He thought the man would stand there in the mirror, even after he was gone.

Shirl was waiting for him outside the door.

"You'll have ice at your place," she said, as she took his arm. "You carry the bottle. I don't want to look like a whore."

"No," he said angrily. He stopped her, put both his hands on her shoulders. He could not see her clearly. "Don't you say a thing like that again." He took the sack from her and guided her to the door.

"It was a joke," she said, as he pushed open the swinging doors for her.

Sam squinted at the light. Fading daylight. He was astonished. How many hours, days had he been in the bar? He looked at his watch. It was only nine o'clock. Still light in Winnemucca. He blinked.

"It doesn't get dark here till about ten in the summer," Shirl said and touched his arm.

They walked along the sidewalk in silence, the sound of her heels the only noise he was aware of though the traffic passed in the street to his side. They stepped around the dirty puddle of melted ice cream. The sight of the family standing around the dropped cone darting into Sam's mind and away again. He thought he reeled a little but steadied his gaze to straight ahead. He concentrated on the squares of the sidewalk. The candy wrappers in the gutter.

A procession of seven cars with camping gear and

suitcases, and small trailers attached, moved quietly down the street. To each bumper was tied a yellow banner that read "Jehovah's Witnesses, Conference." A little boy with short hair waved at them from a station wagon. The air was warm and dry and there was not even a hint of a breeze. Cars pulling trailers passed. Campers, motor homes. Summer on the move. The trees along the sidewalk were dusty again already.

"People driving all night. That's the way to get across this desert," Shirl said.

They turned in at Sam's motel. They walked along the sidewalk by the pool. People were swimming and splashing and shouting. Sam felt the key in his pocket. He had trouble getting it in the lock. He had to check the room number. He thought he might have it wrong. Shirl was staring curiously at his station wagon. She seemed about to ask him something.

"Jump, jump," a child called.

"It's noisy," Sam murmured.

The room was cool; the light showing through the white drapes, the voices and water noise from the pool were filtered and sounded far away. Sam put the bottle on the dresser.

"Do you want a drink?" he asked.

"Not yet," she said, coming toward him. "Is that your . . ."

With a desire that exploded like pain in his body, he reached for her. She did not have a chance to ask him about the girl who had left the note.

He remembered unzipping her dress. He remembered the feel of her skin as he slipped the dress down over her body. His vision began to blur when she turned to face him. He did not recognize her. He saw her breasts and his hands moved automatically to them, but though he knew he must be touching them, they seemed to vanish, to dissolve beneath his clumsy grasp.

They moved to the bed. She led him, he supposed. The light making the drapes stark white blinded him. He saw only silhouettes against the brightness. White and blazing like the salt flats, taking away his vision. Was it only this morning? He saw himself bend and remove his shoes. He undressed, and he watched himself from the mirror. He could not seem to see the woman in bed, dark against the sheets, eyes closed, waiting for him. His own body seemed dusky, almost black. The bed was cool, where it touched his side, like water. He moved his hand down the woman's body. He knew that was what he was doing. He started at her throat, drawing a wide line down her middle. But when his hand slipped onto the sheets, he did not feel the difference. A terror that the bed was empty, that there was no woman, struck him and he reached for her with both arms.

Yes, she was there; he could feel her elbows, her knees. The bones were there, but what about the flesh?

She cooed into his ear. "Honey," she whispered.

She moved against him like water, soft waves of water. He could not locate his hands. She guided him with fingers that were hard and strong. He could not connect his thoughts with his body. He was all flesh and she was all bone. He could not move.

"Come on," she urged. "Please, honey, come on . . ."

There was too much light. He could not see at all now. His fingers warm and moist, safe in his pocket. No. Were his eyes closed? She moaned quietly. She sounded far away. But no, she was attached to his hand. She was growing out of his hand. His body ached and his legs would not move.

"Now," she whispered, and he reached for where he thought she must be. She must be there beside him.

Thelma wasn't home. Katy, where was Katy? Standing by the roadside in the rain. Raindrops washing away her face. Where was the woman? What was her name? He could call her name, in all this sunlight, and she would block the rays, and he would be able to see again.

He thought he must be on top of her. But it was no different from the dream. He felt a sharp pain at his back. A scratch in the flesh, jagged.

"Okay, Sam," she whispered. "Okay."

She was still there. If he could find the place; couldn't she tell he needed help? Sharp hands, bony hands, running down his belly, catching in the hair on his chest, tangling and pushing. He was lost.

And then, as if eclipsed by his cry, the light was gone. The room was dark. Shirl moaned. He thought she said, "No. Wait." Too late.

There were voices outside his room. Someone jumped into the pool with a yell. A splash. Laughter. People walking on the sidewalk, talking, shoes scraping the concrete.

Shirl rubbed against his leg. "It's all right," she said, "don't worry."

He did not understand. It was some time before he felt the stickiness on his stomach, the wetness around his groin. He thought the water from the pool had somehow . . . no. The sheets were cold and damp, the room humid and nearly dark.

"Everyone out of the pool," a man called. "Ten o'clock."

Sam guessed he should say he was sorry, but he had no idea how to form the words.

He managed to get out of bed and walk to the bathroom. Inside, under the harsh yellow light above the mirror, he ran water on his face. He dampened a towel and washed at his stomach without looking. He stared at his face in the mirror, at the lines, the eyes that were red and trembling. The man in the mirror was terrified. He could smell it. The fear scented the air.

From the bedroom came small noises. Yes, he reminded himself, she was still there. He hoped she would dress and leave, close the door with a delicate click. But she did not.

He opened the door. He could hear short breathing, the slightest sound of movement in the bed. He squinted in the near darkness. He could see her moving underneath the sheet. Her breathing increased. Sam stood watching. He wondered if he was now the man in the mirror. Was he there, in that bed with her? No. He felt the hair prickle at the back of his neck. A chill descended his arms. He was cold, nearly to the point of shaking. And he could not take his eyes off the woman's form that moved gently, but with increasing momentum in the bed. Now she moaned in rhythmic tones, faster. Sam knew that tears blurred his vision. He put his hands out in front of him. He wanted to stop her, to stop himself.

Then with a short soft cry, she was still. Her breathing became long even strokes in the night. An arm, dark against the pillow, emerged from beneath the sheets. She seemed to nestle flat into the bed. The room was completely quiet.

Sam stepped back into the bathroom and closed the door. He was hypnotized by the reflection in the mirror. He thought of the gun in the glove box. He had been carrying that gun for a reason. And there were hundreds of miles of deserted roads. He searched the eyes in the mirror for a flicker of recognition, and there was none.

He opened the glass door and turned the shower on. The sound of the water beating against the tile walls scattered his thoughts. Wanting to drown, he stepped into the stream. The noise was overwhelming. There, in the comfort of the storm, he leaned his head against the wall and sobbed. There, with the water catching in his hair, he wept for all his losses. He wept because he would not use the gun on himself any more than Thelma would splatter the tile in the bathroom with her own blood.

And in the room, the woman slept soundly. There were no more splashing sounds from the pool. In the room next to Sam's, the little boy who had been afraid to jump sat quietly, tears glistening in his eyes, while his mother tied a string of dental floss around a hopelessly loose tooth.

The service station inspector locked the door to his room, slipped the key into his pocket, and started for the casinos and a couple of hours of entertainment.

It was dark enough to see some stars.

Nine to ten was the slowest time. Too late for dinner pizza, too early for the late night snack. Even the cowboys, pushing and shoving and jostling about, had departed. Katy and Dinah sat at the table near the kitchen door and watched for new customers. Katy's feet hurt. Dinah smoked a cigarette. Louie was in the kitchen, and George washed glasses behind the bar.

But the pain in Katy's stomach had subsided.

> "She drives her bus at dusk
> With headlights off
> And headphones up
> And for tomorrow
> She has planned a shopping spree."

Phoebe Snow was big in Winnemucca.

"You going to stay awhile?" Dinah asked. "I mean, is this a permanent temporary summer job, as Louie calls it."

"I was on my way home," Katy said. "But," she paused and looked at George behind the bar. "Do you think Louie'd hire me for a month or so?"

"Probably till September; that's when the tourist trade, or as Louie calls it, the captive travelers, stranded overnight in Winnemucca, heart of the Golden West, evaporates." Dinah drew on her cigarette. She had painted fingernails. Katy looked at her own nails. She put her hands under the table.

"Where do you live?" Katy asked her.

"I have an apartment down around the corner, up a block," Dinah said.

"I might ask him if I could stay and work awhile."

"He pays slave wages, but he's fun," Dinah added. "And he's a terrific lover, and he's mine." She laughed.

Katy smiled, remembering frame houses along the street. Yellow, pink, white. Rain-washed. Dinah and Louie would probably live in one someday. A yard. A garden. Bright green grass and sparkling drops of water on windowpanes. Sun making steam from the roof of a home in Winnemucca. She wondered if Louie and Dinah would have a baby. Maybe more than one. Dinah was a lucky girl to have Louie.

"You ladies can go in the back for a while if you want," Louie said. He stood by the side of their table and looked down at Dinah. "Pretty slow tonight. Only the religious orders have saved us." He raised his hands over his head. "Hallelujah, brother, praise the Lord." He wiggled his fingers, shook his pelvis, clapped his hands.

Katy cleared her throat. "Louie? Am I doing all right? Except for that one pizza, I mean?"

"You're doing just fine, Katy, fine indeed," Louie said.

"Thanks." She smiled at him. She could see him in a house in Winnemucca. See him mowing the lawn. Playing with a baby in a playpen. She could see George, too, tossing a dark-haired little boy into the air, catching him, laughing.

"There is just one thing, sweetheart," he leaned down in mock seriousness. "I got to warn you about these cowpokes . . ."

"Louie," Dinah cautioned.

"I mean it. When a good old boy offers to let you ride his horse, you got to be sure you understand what horse he is talking about. You see?"

Katy blushed.

"I mean, they'll kid you and all, you just laugh it off. Mostly they're just talk anyway, but they're going to keep after you for a time." Louie was no longer smiling.

A gnarled old man walked up behind Louie and hit him on the shoulder with his cane.

"You," said the man in a scratchy voice, "You, boy . . . you."

Louie turned. "Hello, Mr. Antonelli. How are you this fine evening?"

"I didn't get my newspaper. All this week, I didn't get my newspaper. I look in bushes, everywhere. No paper." Mr. Antonelli poked at Louie's chest with the red rubber tip of his cane. "What you do with my paper?"

"Mr. Antonelli, I don't deliver papers anymore. I don't even know who your paperboy is now. You ask your daughter."

"I see you on bicycle. You go right by my house."

"It wasn't me," Louie protested, and he reached out to take Mr. Antonelli's arm. "Come on."

Mr. Antonelli cracked Louie hard on the wrist with his cane, and Louie yelped.

Dinah stood and Katy stared.

"Mr. Antonelli," Dinah said softly. "Does your daughter know where you are?"

"What?" he asked, and he turned his gaze to Katy. He wore thick small glasses, and his black eyes glistened behind the lenses. His mouth began to tremble. He put his cane to the floor and leaned on it. Moving his eyes from face to face, he questioned them silently. He did not know where he was, that much was clear.

"Come on, Mr. Antonelli, I'll walk you down to the corner to your daughter's place, okay?" Louie's face was filled with compassion.

The little old man who seemed dazed murmured something that no one understood and let himself be led from the Pizza Place by the proprietor.

"Poor thing," Katy said to Dinah.

"He's always mixed up," Dinah replied.

Back through the door like dancers who know only one number came the cowboys.

"My hell," one of them said. "You should see what old man Kristopoulis has got going at his place."

"Whooee," yelled another. He put his hands above his head and began to swivel his hips. His boots made loud hollow sounds on the wooden floor. The jukebox was silent, and the snickers, the hand smacking, clapping echoed in Mr. Antonelli's absence, louder than before.

"Settle down," said Dinah.

"There's a place in France, where the women wear no pants," sang cowboy Cale in the nasal tone of the mystical snake dance. "This woman, she is damned near naked, and she came right by our table, and old Willy, he got so excited he damned near peed his pants. I tucked a dollar bill right in her crack." Shouts and catcalls, laughter, noise. "Beer, beer, give me beer," they sang to George.

The four cowboys arranged themselves into a disorderly line at the bar. They were constant motion.

"What exactly are you boys talking about?" George asked in a formal tone.

"Old man Kristo's got a belly dancer over there, that's what," the cowboy in the red shirt said. "A real live, damned near naked belly dancer with gold coins hanging all over her tits."

Louie came through the door and shouted, "Keep it

down, will you?" and while the cowboys stared at him, he pushed past them into the kitchen.

"Well, hooey to you . . ." and Cale raised a finger at the kitchen door.

Dinah and Katy both followed Louie.

"What happened? Did you get him home?" Dinah asked.

"Sure," Louie said. He stirred a pot of sauce on the stove and didn't look at them. "Fatso, we're closing early tonight. Start cleaning up."

"What happened?" Dinah repeated.

Louie put the spoon down and leaned against the counter. "That poor old bugger," he said. "All the way home, he's telling me that no one's taking care of the cemetery, the grass is all brown, the flowers are all dead. He's talking about his wife's grave and some of his kids, and then he turns to me and asks me why I've stopped taking care of the cemetery. Why am I so lazy, why don't I pull the weeds, water the grass?"

Louie folded his arms.

"So hell, I get him home, he doesn't know who I am, who he is, nothing, and Mrs. Vincenza has fallen asleep in front of the TV. She doesn't even know he's been gone till I wake her up . . ."

"It was good you took him back," Dinah said, and she walked to him, kissed him on the cheek, leaned against him.

"Then she stands there right in front of him. Christ, she's tired too, and sad. She says she has to watch him every second, he's like a baby, like a little tiny baby, how can she watch him every second? She supposed to chain him to the chair?"

"The poor old man," Katy said. She placed her hand on the lower right side of her stomach.

"It must be shit to get so damned old," Louie said.

"The alternative isn't so hot either," Dinah added.

"I don't see how it can be worse." Louie took off his apron.

"There's a belly dancer at the place across from the Star," George said as he came through the swinging doors.

"Great," Louie said. "We're closing early, and we will just go over there and tie one on." Fatso began to put away the trays of chopped pepper and onion.

"Let's clean up out front," Dinah said to Katy.

The cowboys with hats intact were still at the bar. Dinah directed Katy, telling her what had to be done in order to close up. A middle-aged couple came through the door and Dinah said, "Sorry, we're not serving anyone else tonight."

They nodded, looked at each other, then at the four young men at the bar. The man held the door for the woman as they stepped back out into the Winnemucca summer night.

"That goes for you boys, too," Dinah said, "Drink up, we're closing early."

"We see belly dancing a lot in Berkeley," Katy said. "A friend of my mother's even took lessons."

"You're kidding," said Dinah as she wiped off the table where the Jehovah's Witnesses had been.

"It's kind of an arty thing to do. Lots of symbolism. Phyllis talked about it constantly. That's my mother's friend. She was always into new stuff."

"I can just see my mother," Dinah said, "all two hundred and fifty pounds of her."

"The Greeks like heavy women," Katy said. "At least Phyllis said so."

Katy picked up a napkin off the floor and crumpled it into a ball. The residual knock of the past pain in her side produced a tiny throb.

The cowboys were talking quietly, but when Katy

turned she could see they were watching her in the mirror. One nudged another in the ribs, sending a wave of vibration through all four. Snickers. They were talking about her.

"Something the matter?" George asked.

"No. Yes. Those guys get on my nerves," Katy whispered.

George shrugged, and Katy did not know whether he agreed with her or not, and taking the tray of salt and pepper, he went back into the kitchen.

Two teenage girls in white shorts and halter tops came through the door, and Dinah said, "No more pizza tonight. We're closing early for a change."

The girls smiled shyly, glanced at the four young men at the bar, and left.

Katy was straightening the chairs in the corner when Dinah turned off the lights in the restaurant. Now the only illuminated portion was the stretch of bar and the white-hatted cowboys.

"Hurry up," Dinah said to them as she went into the kitchen.

Katy didn't hear him come up behind her. Suddenly an arm went around her waist and pulled her against him.

"It's time for that ride," a voice whispered in her ear, and she could smell the sour odor of beer on his breath. She looked frantically at the bar and three hats lined up there, the faces too dark to identify.

"Let me go," she said, struggling. The pain, like a snip from sharp scissors, made her stop still. The cowboy's arm was hard and rope-tight strong. He nuzzled into her neck, and she felt a wet mouth, the tip of his tongue behind her ear.

"Let me go," she said, and the stick of pain hit again so sharply that she gasped. "Please let me go."

"Give a cowboy one little kiss."

"No. Let go, or I'll yell."

And then, as if the game was one of dare, the cowboy grabbed Katy's breasts. She screamed first in amazement; then, in pain she shrieked. Both Louie and George bolted into the room, the swinging padded doors from the kitchen thudding in the wind.

"Let her go," George shouted, and he pulled at the cowboy.

He released Katy with such abruptness, she fell into the table, banging her leg against the chair. A gasping sob rose in her throat, and she did not hear the commotion in the bar above the roar in her head.

Louie was herding the cowboys out, threatening them, shouting at them. George, with the grace of a bouncer, had the miscreant's arm twisted in back of him, and he steered him wincing with pain toward the door.

"Shit, you dumb fucker," Louie said. "You stupid pricks, get the hell out and sober yourselves up. I should call the cops."

Louie's rage was deep and cold and circled the room with fury. The cowboys, splashed with the icy water of anger, stumbled from the Pizza Place on awkward calf-like legs.

George, for the second time in one day, put his arms around a sobbing Katy.

"Hey, it's all right," he whispered. "Come on, they're gone." He stroked her hair.

Louie kicked a chair halfway across the room and slammed past Dinah into the kitchen. Dinah locked the front door. Katy cried quietly with George's arms around her. She thought he might kiss her, but he did not.

"Dammit," she said. "Why do these things keep happening?"

"In an hour and a half, this day will be over. New day, new start. Okay?"

"Okay," she smiled. The pain in her stomach was gone. All that remained was the faint bruise of feeling. She put her arms around George and hugged him.

"All right," Louie said, "enough is enough, folks." He grinned, but didn't seem happy. "We are going to see the jingle, jangle, jingle of the lady with the golden coins. We will watch the erotic contorting of her body, and we will be happy." He bowed. "And before we go, in the privacy of our own home, we will share in the ancient delights of a carefully rolled joint."

Dinah slipped her arms around his waist. "Yes," she whispered.

"The belly dancer comes on again at eleven-thirty," George said.

"We'll get there just in time," Louie announced. Then he began to sing; quick little dance steps accompanied the words. Dinah laughed. George shook his head.

"Just in time, I found you just in time, before you came my time was running low." Tap, shuffle, stamp. "I was lost, the losing dice was tossed, my bridges all were crossed, nowhere to go . . ."

Old songs, new songs, altogether singing against the discrepancies in the streets of Winnemucca.

And even the disasters were part of the cloth, the mistakes that said "handmade with care." High spots, low spots, set into the rhythm. A crumpled pizza on the floor, stained with tears.

Katy took a small box from the pocket inside her pack. She stood before the mirror in the bathroom and looked at the color of her own eyes. They were green and young, not old and shiny black with age. She removed the small gold stud earrings and inserted the delicate dangling stars in her ears. She shook her head to see them tremble in the light.

When she rejoined her new friends, they did not notice the change.

When Sam went back into the bedroom, the woman was asleep. She had not, as he prayed she would, left silently in the night. She stretched slim in the bed, quiet underneath the blue-white sheets, and Sam did not want to wake her.

He wondered if she heard him sobbing in the shower, and decided she had not. Certainly, had she known she would have gone away. People left you alone with your grief. Give them time, give them time to adjust, alone. That had not worked either. All that aloneness.

He wondered if he could call Thelma without waking the woman and decided he could not. The only sound in the room was the soft whirr of the air conditioner.

He hoped he never would have to see the woman again. He imagined the cold scornful look in her eyes. He could not bear the thought.

He dressed soundlessly. He had trouble with the buttons on his shirt. His mind was still not in sync with his hands. The drapes formed a large blue square, their eerie whiteness gone at last. Everything was over. He hoped, when he left the room, he would be able to see the stars in the sky.

He finished dressing, took a last look at his hair in the bathroom mirror, and avoided the gaze of the man who inhabited his body. He closed the door with a controlled soft click. She would not wake.

Outside he stared up at the sky. He put his hands in his pockets and leaned his head back. The sky was brilliant black. Shiny, hard, dense. The stars were perfectly white lights, flickering. An infinite bowl turned upside down. Wishes and prayers came back, sliding down the sides, whirling into the mind with the waning track of a shooting star.

He looked for the Big Dipper though it was not his favorite. He took a deep breath. The air was cooler now. And the moisture was gone. Dry summer night in Winnemucca. And all the stars were there. He found the Big Dipper and counted the points. Then he searched.

Sam had loved Orion from the time he was a boy. He could, if the giant was there, locate him every time. He would trace the three stars in Orion's girdle with a pointed finger in the night.

See. That's the one. No look, those three stars in a row, see there. That's Orion. He's a giant. See his belt. Julianna, head back, straining to see. *Where Daddy? Point your finger right where to look.* Down on his knees to see her angle of vision, down on his knees in the grass. Dew wet grass at home. He was so much bigger than she was. He was the giant, the Orion. *There. I see it. I see it, Daddy.* And then they would move, finger tracing across the sky, looking for Sirius, the dog. Orion's dog. *See how bright that one is, Juli? See?* She could not always find the dog. And she could not always count the seven sisters. But then, of course, Sam thought as he stood in front of the motel in Winnemucca, there weren't really seven stars. There were only six. One of the seven sisters hid, the story went, she hid in the black night sky in grief, or in shame. He could not remember, the stories were so old, told to him so long ago.

But maybe, Sam thought, and the tears made glowing halos around the brightest stars, the seventh sister had died. Why didn't they admit it? Somewhere in the centuries past, the seventh sister had simply died.

He had to admit it, too. He had to face it. Julianna was gone, just like the seventh sister. He could look at the sky every night for all time, and that star would never again appear.

And Orion was not there. Sam laughed at the irony. No one was where they were supposed to be. Not even the giant. Summer, yes, in summer Orion appeared near dawn. Wasn't that something to have forgotten.

He would cry again if he did not stop. He started toward the sidewalk. He could use a drink. He cleared his throat. The cars went by slowly in the street. The faces of the travelers were turned yellow by the insect-repellent street lamps. Cars with racks on top, sleeping bags, tents, looking for cooler country in which to camp. People in back seats with pillows holding their sleeping heads. A driver in a short-sleeved shirt, drumming his fingers on the steering wheel while he waited for the light to change. A man and a woman in identical checkered shirts came toward him on the sidewalk. They held hands. They nodded and smiled and the man said, "Good evening."

Sam hurried along to Kristo's place. He was consumed with a need to explain to someone and Kristo was the only person left. The stars frightened him now. He knew that out on one of those desolate Nevada roads, he would be able to see them all. There would be no trees to filter the light, no barely moving leaves, no noise. The stars would be white hot pinpricks and they would scare him to death in the silence. Out in the desert, a cold metal gun in his hand, he would be frightened into oblivion.

He looked at his watch as he walked. Another hour to go in what seemed an impossibly long day. The last hours had been wrenched from him, painfully pulled out by their bloody roots. He put his hand to his chest.

Ahead, the neon lights beckoned, and Sam felt strong enough to run, but was wise enough not to begin. A man running along the street means trouble. The sound of running footsteps on the pavement. Emergency.

He saw the network of bright bulbs that formed the front of the Star Broiler. A bulb was burned out. One of the seven sisters was missing. Sam rubbed his temple and thought how nice it would be to have a drink.

Inside the door, the woman at the cashier stand looked surprised. She opened her mouth as if to ask a question, then smiled in a stiff way.

"Kristo's upstairs in his office," she said, before Sam could ask.

The music was not playing. The band must be taking a break, Sam thought, as he turned to the stairs. He wanted, for some reason, to hear the sound of the bouzouki tuning, the rhythm of the drums. Anything that said life was going to continue. He paused and said to the woman, "How was the show? How did the dancer do?"

"Well, it was different," the woman said. She looked disapproving.

Four young men came into the club. They wore white hats and cowboy clothes, and they were laughing too loud, and talking too loud.

"When's the next show?" the cowboy in the red shirt demanded as he pounded a fist on the counter in front of the cashier.

"Bring on the babe with the jingling tits," said another.

Sam listened to the protests of the cashier. He thought he heard her call a man's name as he mounted the stairs to Kristo's office.

"I tell you when I grabbed that skinny chick, there wasn't nothing there."

Sam sneered at the cowboys, at their youth, at their energy. The bitterness he ached to dispel soured his mouth and he thought with anticipation that life would treat those boys badly. Eventually something would happen to kill their freedom and their disregard.

He knocked on the door of Kristo's office. *I never told you. My daughter died two months ago.* The words were ready, and then it would be all over. He turned the knob and entered.

Sitting in the chair where Shirl had been earlier, was the belly dancer. She smoked a cigarette and looked calmly at Sam with eyes that were shaded dark green from the lid to the eyebrow. She was all gold and green and rounded pale flesh. She wore rings and arm bracelets, and the coins shimmered around her breasts and the low slung band that held chiffon to make a skirt.

"Where's Shirl?" Kristo asked.

Sam stared at the soft mound of flesh that surrounded the dancer's navel.

"She was tired," he said, his mouth dry. He wanted to tell Kristo the truth, but not in front of the woman in the gold coins and chiffon. The slight motion of moving the cigarette to and from her lips caused the coins to tinkle.

"This is Magda," Kristo said. "I told you about my new act."

"Sam." He extended his hand, then withdrew it. "How did the show go?"

"Great," Kristo said. "Had them falling in the aisles.

We've got some class after all, here in Winnemucca." He smiled.

"You want a drink?" he asked Sam, and pointed to a chair.

"Bourbon and water, a double," Sam said.

"That good, eh?" Kristo smiled and winked.

The woman rustled the coins and stared. Inhaling, exhaling, her bosom pushing and overflowing the tight coin-studded cups.

Kristo used the intercom to order the drinks.

She ground out the cigarette and everything moved. Her earrings, the flesh at the top of her arm, her hair. Long eyelashes, thick and false, fluttered. The coins turned light in odd directions.

"The band," said Magda, "is okay. You coming down for this show?" She stood and smoothed down the chiffon scarves. She lifted, from the back of the chair, a large square piece of blue silk edged in gold and draped it around her body.

A waitress brought in a tray with a bottle of bourbon, a bucket of ice, and two glasses.

"We'll be down later," Kristo said.

Sam wondered at the carefulness of Kristo's gaze, of his words. A man with gray-silk control. Magda looked at him seductively, and Kristo stared back, a current between them that excluded Sam.

She passed Sam, and he thought of a silver poplar tree and the long line of them, trees whose leaves rustled green and silver, round like the coins. A confusing sight. The woman, the dancer, was not at all like a tree and the memory struck Sam as inappropriate.

"So what happened, Sam?" Kristo asked as soon as the door closed behind Magda. He poured the drinks as he spoke.

Sam stood and took one of the glasses of straight bourbon. He brushed away Kristo's offer of water.

"It didn't work," he said. "Sorry. She's back at my place asleep."

"Didn't work?" Kristo asked.

"I let her down," Sam said coldly. "My mind, something went funny."

"I see," said Kristo. "Your mind."

"My wife isn't home. I'm worried," Sam said.

"Infidelity is easier for some than for others," Kristo said. He leaned forward in his chair. He was concerned, Sam could tell. "You want to call her from here?" he asked.

"No. I know she's all right," Sam lied. He took a deep drink of the bourbon, flinched as the strength of the alcohol burned his throat, and tried to dispel the aura of trouble. "There are a million and one places she might be. She didn't expect me till tomorrow anyway."

"You call if you want."

Sam shook his head. He was sorry he'd used that as an excuse. If something was wrong, he didn't want to know it. What could he do anyway? What had he ever been able to do?

The alcohol warmed him inside with a great rush. He felt the tightness in his arms begin to loosen.

Kristo leaned back as if the crisis had passed. "Don't worry about Shirl," he said. "She's a big girl; she can take care of herself."

"Do you know anything about the stars, Kristo?" Sam asked as he stood and filled his glass with bourbon. He dropped in an ice cube that felt electric with the cold on his fingers. "Anything about constellations, I mean."

"Some," Kristo said. "I know because I know mythology. I studied it, Greek art, the paintings, the sculpture. You need to know it to understand."

"When Julianna was little, we used to sit outside at night and look for the stars. You know, the Big Dipper, the Little Dipper. Damned hard to find the Little Dipper. Damned hard." Sam took another drink.

"I don't often look for stars in the sky, I have to admit," Kristo said. "I haven't thought about it for a long while. I don't know why I don't look anymore."

"Orion, that's the one we could always find. Orion, chasing his seven daughters." Sam sniffed. "But there are only six. Did you know that, Kristo? They call them seven sisters and there's only six." He thought for a moment that he slurred his words. But it was impossible. Second drink. His tongue was clumsy, that was all. He blinked, clearing his vision.

"Oh, they aren't his daughters," Kristo said. "You are mixed up there." He smiled. "But it's an easy mistake to make."

"I thought they were his daughters," Sam repeated. Again he had trouble with the words. Was there something wrong with his drink? He could see the flashing lights from the Star Broiler and Casino across the street in back of Kristo's head. His hand tightened on the glass. "Who were they if they weren't his daughters?"

"They were the daughters of Atlas," Kristo said. "Orion chased them because he was in love with them. We are not so different today, do you think, Sam, in the way we chase?" He laughed and raised his glass in a toast.

In the background, Sam heard the music begin. It was a faint melody at first, then increased in volume. The distinctive sounds of the Macedonian instruments moved into his consciousness and he said, "The show must be starting."

"Yes," said Kristo. "We can go down later. What did you want to say about Orion, about the hunter?"

"What happened to Orion's daughter?" Sam asked, then felt the blood rise in his face. "Did he have daughters? Maybe he didn't. I don't know about mythology. I thought the seven sisters were his daughters."

"He had daughters," Kristo said. "They sacrificed themselves, I can't remember why." He paused, rubbing his chin. "They were weavers, and they pierced their throats with their shuttles. Then they were turned into comets. As a reward."

The bourbon burned in Sam's stomach. His vision was dimmed and the face of Kristo faded into the sky that seemed to come in through the window and encompass Sam. He blinked. Had he almost blacked out? He pushed himself up from the chair and steadied himself against the desk. He poured more bourbon into the glass, and reached into the ice bucket for another cube. He had to think about this. Comets.

"Yes," Kristo added, nodding his head, "two virgins sacrificed and turned into comets . . . by Pluto I think. Yes." He seemed pleased with his knowledge.

"Kristo," Sam said as he stood before the man's desk. "Kristo, two months ago my Julianna died. She was only fifteen years old. She died on her birthday. Can you imagine that? She died on her fifteenth birthday."

He thought he spoke quietly. He didn't really know. He hoped he wasn't yelling or crying; he hoped he wasn't being a fool. "You see, Kristo," Sam said, "I thought Orion was chasing his daughters . . . maybe they had disobeyed him, I don't know."

Was he crying? He could not feel tears.

Kristo stood and came around to him. The look of pleasure was gone from his face. His eyes were small black pellets filled with pain for his friend. He put his arm around Sam.

"You should have told me, Sam. You should have told me sooner."

Sam leaned, his palms on the desk. No, there were no tears in his eyes. The lights were all clear and cold and perfectly set. Nothing flickered, wavered, haloed, or blurred. As clear and as cold as the sacred loneliness.

"How did this happen, Sam? Sit down here, tell me how such a thing could happen?"

"She had a tumor," Sam said as he moved back to the black leather chair. "It grew in her brain so fast nothing could be done."

And in his mind, he saw comets trailing across the sky. Blood red comets. He heard the words he spoke to Kristo from a distance, maybe even as far away as the music from the Macedonian band. All those years he thought the seven sisters were the daughters of Orion. All those years he had been wrong about a lot of things. He told the story of his daughter's death with a certain lack of interest. After all, he had heard it before. He knew. He knew when he spoke of Thelma, how she looked at him. To Kristo, he said merely that she seemed to blame him. Kristo nodded. Sam thought he understood.

"There are no answers, Sam," he said once. "You love someone, the someone dies. It is impossible to understand why."

Sam looked at his hands as he spoke. "It's different. Julianna's death. See, I keep thinking she's lost. Not dead. Lost. And that I can find her." He paused, rubbing his knuckles. "Like she's run away. Or on the road somewhere like the girl I gave a ride. Katy. I can't get it through my head."

"Maybe it's too soon," Kristo said. "Just give 'it time."

Sam could hear the music from the Macedonian band.

"But see, Kristo, I feel like I'm *about* to find her. I know that's not possible, but that's what I keep feeling."

Sam talked quietly now, almost to himself. "When my mother died, it was different. She was old. I had more to remember about her. Sundays when I was a kid, how she cried when Thelma and I got married. See, it seems like in a way she's still with me. Juli is just gone."

"Your little Juli didn't have so much time to make a memory, Sam."

"I know."

"I mean time to create a memory for you. All the things you think you should remember about a person's life. Hers . . . like an unfinished song. You've got to make some kind of song out of what you have. A dance, like those that we old men do. A dance in a line. Hers will be different."

Kristo leaned back in his chair and never took his eyes from Sam's face.

"Maybe"—he went on—"you think your Juli was your immortality."

Sam shook his head.

"And what if I lusted after my own daughter?"

"Ah, Sam. Sometimes our love plays little tricks on us. Sends us wrong signals. Love would not be immortal if it were simple. You loved your Juli. You just didn't have enough time."

Time. So the two men sat in Kristopoulis's office. The traffic went by in the street, the lights from the Star Broiler burned white against the night, the Macedonian band played while Magda danced. Once, in contrast to his memories, Sam heard a yell that must have come from the club below. Then another rebel cry. He saw Magda, green and gold and jangling, her flesh stark white against the floor.

"One more time to tell her I love her."

"You can whisper it, and you can think it," Kristo said. "She will know it."

"I need to hear the sound of her voice again."

"You'll have to weave it into the memory then," Kristo said, leaning forward on his desk, folding his hands.

A song, a whisper, a dance in a line. Orion crossing the sky seeking stars, a little girl in the dew wet grass looking up. Sam searched for the melody, trying to draw it out and away from the music that could be heard from the club. The Seven Sisters. Daughters, mothers, wives.

And all the while, the constellations whirled in confusion in his head. He could not count them, or any longer, remember their names.

"Sometimes," Louie said as he passed the joint to George, "I think I ought to throw in my gourmet's towel and open up a dancing school."

The four of them sat crosslegged on the rug.

"You'll have to find your gourmet first," George cracked.

"You would be great on television," Katy said. "Maybe the Johnny Carson show."

"Seriously, cuz," Louie continued.

The joint was perched gracefully between Dinah's lips, and she took a deep hit.

"The lure of the stage, the tinsel, the lights. Once you've had a taste of stardom." Louie looked reverently heavenward.

Katy inhaled the smoke from the joint, held it in her lungs for a moment, then exhaled.

"We could teach the tap, jazz, stuff like that," Louie said. "Dinah here had some ballet lessons, didn't you, babe?"

"Right," Dinah said. "I'm a real ballerina. I was a dancing flower in the school production of Snow White and the Seven Dwarfs. It wasn't exactly the lead."

"But you were sensational," Louie leered at her. "Come into my bedroom, I make you a star, *sveethard*."

"What will Katy teach?" George asked. He put his hand on her knee.

"Katy knows something about belly dancing," Dinah volunteered.

"Right," Katy said, passing the joint. "I'm an expert on belly dancing." She produced a stiff laugh.

"Are we going to Kristo's?" Dinah asked.

"All in good time, my sweet, all in good time," Louie nuzzled at the back of Dinah's neck.

George held the joint out to him.

"Listen, kids," Louie said, without noticing. "Why don't the two of you go on over to Kristo's and get a table. We'll be over in a while. How does that sound, George. Okay?"

"Louie," said Dinah.

"Fine," said George. He got to his feet. "Come on," he said to Katy.

When he pulled her up, she gasped and placed her hand at the center of her stomach.

"Sorry," George said. He looked puzzled.

"It's okay," she said as she bit her lip.

"See you there," she said to Dinah and Louie. George took her hand.

Outside on the street, they paused and looked up at the sky.

"I'll bet you can see the stars better in Nevada than any other state," Katy said.

"That's because we work so cheap."

Katy was bewildered. He laughed and put his arm around her shoulders. "Sorry, I knew what you meant." He too, looked up. "I guess I'm used to it," he said. "I've lived here all my life."

All trace of the rain was gone. The sky was black and the stars were perfectly clear. Millions of them dotted the sky, more than Katy had ever seen, more than she knew existed.

"Wonder where those people are by now that gave us a ride?"

"Probably saying their prayers," George said.

"Does Dinah remind you of Mary Ann?" she asked.

"No."

"Not even a little?"

"No."

"Wonder where Mr. Batinovich is?" She tripped lightly on a broken piece of sidewalk, stumbling against George.

"Far away, I hope."

"Funny," Katy said, "I thought we would see him again."

They walked along a dark sidewalk. There were small frame houses on each side of the street. A single bare hanging bulb lit the intersection. Paint-peeling white fences separated the sidewalk from the yards. It was still warm and there was almost no breeze. They passed before a house where the light from the television screen shone blue through the mesh door. They could not see who watched the show. Johnny Carson's voice crackled into the night. As they walked by the next house, there was a rustle in the bushes and Katy jumped, squeezing George's hand in alarm. A black-and-white cat who stared at them with strange sapphire eyes appeared silently on the fence, blinked at them, jumped in front of them, and ran under a truck that was parked at the curb.

At the corner, under the bare bulb light, was a chain-link enclosed square lot. Several battered automobiles glittered relentlessly and grotesquely in the dark. Spider-webbed windshields, missing doors. Katy walked to the fence and looped her fingers through the wire and tried to see. In the corner, nearest the garage, was the wreckage of a camper. The back wheels were missing and the rear was mangled. She squinted. A jumping trout. Antlers of a stag on the crumpled shell.

"Wow. I wonder what happened to that," Katy said.

"I'd say something smashed into it, myself," George replied, "but that's only a guess."

"Remember that camper with the sign? The funny one?" She tried to see the bumper, or what remained of it. She thought she could see shreds of yellow, the bumper sticker.

"The one that said, 'If this camper's rockin','" she reminded him.

"Most campers look alike," George said.

"I think I can see the sticker . . ."

"Come on," George said, and pulled her away from the fence, "this is depressing."

"Are we going to see the belly dancer?" she asked, although she looked back once again to try to identify the wreckage.

"I thought we'd take a walk first. It's just a little after eleven. Dinah and Louie won't be there for a while."

"They're close, aren't they."

"Yes."

As if the words were a cue, George stopped her, took her face in his hands, and kissed her on the lips. She put her arms around his neck and kissed him back. His hands slipped around, and he pressed her closer to him. She noticed the sound of the crickets, felt a slight breeze behind her. She could feel the bones of his back, and the muscles under his shirt.

A car screeched around the corner, muffler pounding, racketing, engine roaring. The headlight beams crossed and cut the moment. Katy tried to move, and George held her tightly as if he would protect her. The car raced toward them; there was laughter and yelling, and they stood in the light. A beer bottle hit the curb close to where they were and shattered in the night.

"Whooee."

The car passed by, turned at the next corner, and they listened, holding each other, until the outrageous sound was gone.

"There's nothing worse than a bunch of drunken teen-agers," George said into her ear. "I know, because I was one once."

He put his hand low on her back and pressed her against him again. But it was as if two stones separated them, one that surrounded the pain in her stomach, and one she could feel growing in him.

"Shouldn't we go?" she asked.

"No," he whispered, then taking a deep breath, he pulled away from her. "Sure, right," he said.

An insect brushed her face and her hand rose to her neck. She felt the dangling stars in her ears and gave them a little shake. They walked farther on until they came to a small barren park. A jungle gym, a lopsided wooden merry-go-round, and a slippery slide. Steel blue fixtures in the moonlight.

"Let's go down the slide," he said to her.

"I can't," she whispered. "I'm pregnant."

The time, the sound, and the night stopped. Blood rushed to Katy's face, and she closed her eyes. Without understanding, she had created a dream of living in a little frame house with George, in Winnemucca, and now she had ruined it before it began. The baby would have looked like George.

"You're what?" he said at last. He stood with his hands in his pockets facing her. "What did you say?"

"I'm pregnant."

She walked over to the wooden bench that faced the jungle gym. He followed and sat down, but he did not touch her.

"What are you going to do?" he asked.

"I was on my way home. Now, I wonder if Louie will let me work a couple of months." She folded her hands in her lap. "No one is expecting me."

"Where's the guy?" George asked.

"I don't know."

"Hell, you know who it was, don't you?"

"Of course, I know who it was. It's just that I told him and he split."

"He must be a bastard," George said.

"I don't know. I guess he thought I was taking care of it. Sometimes he was in such a hurry."

George was quiet.

"I didn't want to have an abortion," she said. "Anyway, I thought I should tell you." She stared at the bars of the jungle gym. "I thought that was only fair."

"What did you think? I'd catch it?" He paused. "I'm sorry," he whispered, and put his head back and stared up at the sky.

"You probably ought to go on home to your folks. Do they know?"

"No," she said.

"Will they understand?"

She shivered, as if she were cold. "They always do. I think I did this to shock them. Sometimes it would have been better if they'd used a belt, like your grandma did." She didn't believe that. Her parents had tried to be fair with her. It wasn't that they didn't try.

George looked at her suspiciously. "It will probably shock them all right."

"I don't want this baby," Katy cried. "I don't know why I let this happen."

George looked so deeply into her eyes, she had to turn away. She stood up from the bench. "I guess I've made a big mistake, haven't I?" she whispered.

He did not answer. He reached out and took her hand, but the warmth was gone from his grasp. His palm was calloused and his fingers, bone-hard rough.

"Let's go find Dinah and Louie," he said.

They walked, disenchanted, down the sidewalk toward the main street. Neither one of them looked to the stars. They paced their steps evenly, careful not to step on cracks. Their shoes made discordant sounds against the pavement, an unpleasant noise to go with the end of a summer romance.

A river of fatigue ran through Sam's body. The telling of the story had exhausted him. But the bourbon burned his senses alive as he sat in the black leather chair.

Kristo talked about life and death. Sam thought he mainly stared out the window. An emptiness glowed from the Greek's eyes, as threatening as any malice could be, because it was unaccounted for, unidentified.

Sam tried, while Kristo was in the bathroom, to call Thelma. The low echoing rings created their own vacuum in the distance. It did not occur to Sam to hang up the receiver until Kristo finally said, "She must not be there, Sam. She must be staying over with a friend."

Sam thought of Shirl, wondered if she still slept between the damp white sheets. He thought of Magda, dancing below. He thought maybe Thelma had a lover but could not imagine it. Thelma, the bereaved mother. But before Julianna's death . . .

When they went dancing, she would wear the black dress with the red flowers, and paint her eyes. She had her dark thick hair curled at the beauty shop. He could look at her and remember that she was a pretty woman. The black dress with the red flowers. The telephone ringing on the bed stand. Ringing to an empty house, heard by his own empty heart.

And he felt better because he had told Kristo. The

river flowing outward, yes. He could feel the current from the tips of his fingers, yes. He felt better. Kristo's face had the lines now, Kristo's eyes had the sadness.

And in the sky, Sam thought with a smile, Orion chases the seven sisters. They weren't his daughters after all. They were women like Shirl, like Thelma had been when she was younger, like jingling Magda downstairs. Clumsy Orion who would never catch them struggling across the sky, his dog snapping at his heels. Sam thought the image so funny he began to laugh.

"What is it, Sam?" Kristo asked, smiling himself at Sam's laughter.

"That stupid son-of-a-bitch," Sam muttered. "Chasing the girlies, and at his age . . ."

"Let's go down, see Magda dance. You could use a show, Sam," Kristo said. His smile was glittering and false. His eyes were troubled.

"Yes. It's still my birthday," Sam said as he stood. His vision blurred and he steadied himself against the desk. "Thirty more minutes, yes sir, thirty minutes of happy birthday left." He chuckled while the strains of the song welled up in his brain and he began to sing, "Happy Birthday to me, happy birthday to me . . ."

"Come on," Kristo said. "Let's go downstairs."

Right, Sam thought. Take the patient by the arm, lead him down the green-walled halls, an old man in felt slippers that slapped against the asphalt tile floor.

Sam moved his arm though Kristo had not reached for it. The anticipation preceded the movement by too great a time. It did not fit. Sam shook his head. Still laughing, still smiling. Confused by his rhythmically blurred vision.

"Come on," Kristo repeated. "Remember, we're brothers. Isn't that so? Don't we look enough alike to be brothers?"

"Yes," Sam nodded vigorously. "Yes, indeed. I always wanted a brother. What did I have? Sisters. Sisters, sisters, sisters. Seven sisters. Did you know one of them is missing? Just like Thelma, one of them is missing." He laughed and put his hand on Kristo's shoulder.

The green-carpeted stairs looked impossibly steep. Sam grasped the bannister to steady himself. He suppressed another urge to laugh, then giggle like a child. Kristo stepped in front of him and started down.

"Come on," he urged.

Come on, Shirl had said, come on, honey.

And he had, hadn't he? Right. Yes sir, he had. He swallowed, the drink coming to the back of his throat.

Lights everywhere. Bells and music and buzzers. Clinking coins in slot machines, a rumble of voices, bells, jackpots. He saw only pieces as he passed by. He stumbled into a man in a western tie, a bald man who turned and looked at him in annoyance.

"Sorry," mumbled Sam.

Fruit, oranges, cherries, stars and bars. A purple plum whizzed by, another landed by the side. A young woman in a short pink dress jumped up and down and clapped her hands. Bells and buzzers. A phone ringing, no one answering. Sam waded through the gamblers, through the spectators following Kristo. Sam thought he lumbered like an ape, and he wanted to laugh at that, too. Kristo so calm, so cool. Floating in gray through his own casino, into his club, all these bells, and all this noise belonged to him.

He nodded and smiled at people and Sam stumbled behind him. He saw the multishaded red octagons in the carpet, the silver, the rows of chrome machines. He blinked. He opened his eyes wider. He stared into the face of a woman who blocked his path. She was enormous, and she wore little tiny earrings shaped like birds. She did not move.

" 'Scuse me," Sam muttered and leaned back to let her pass. She frowned at him, he thought, but couldn't be sure. He stared at her earrings; bluebirds that hung by their necks from a golden chain.

"She's a big mother," Sam whispered to Kristo, and the Greek grimaced, but took his friend's arm.

At the table, Sam was served a small pot of coffee. Kristo sipped another amber highball. He talked to Sam. He said once again, he wondered about the trip to Europe. Sam listened and burned his mouth on the coffee. He took deep breaths. He asked for ice water.

The man on the bandstand tested his bouzouki, tinkling notes, running up and down the scale. A man with a guitar by his side sat at a table next to the bandstand and spoke earnestly with a platinum blond woman. The drummer looked vacantly out at the crowd from his perch, waiting to begin again. Magda was not there. Sam looked around the room, letting his eyes skip places, then reconsidering, back and forth.

"Where's Magda?" he said to Kristo.

"She waits off stage. She likes to make an entrance, you know. They play for a while, then she comes on, then she goes off, they play some more. It works pretty good." Kristo raised his hand and signaled to the man who played the bouzouki. He nodded. The drummer called to the man with the guitar. Sam could see all of it, but couldn't figure out exactly what it meant. Then the three men in black shirts and black pants were on the small bandstand. Two of them had mustaches. The drummer looked pale and sunless; his hair was ordinary brown. He hit the cymbal lightly with the brush.

There was a commotion near the back of the room. The band stopped tuning, stopped adjusting the knobs on the amplifiers. Everyone turned to see two large men escorting a young cowboy from the room. He wore a red shirt, and he was cursing. His hat was knocked from his head; he flailed helplessly against the two men, kicking with pointed boots.

"Get my goddamned hat," he shouted. "Somebody pick up my fucking hat."

The three disappeared through the door. A rustle of comment. "Feeling his oats, young snapper, he's a colt, yes sir, kicking up his heels, kicked 'em a little too high. The bulls got him, hell, I'm glad I'm not young like that anymore. No goddamned sense." The sentences, the words, said by the ladies and gentlemen that surrounded the stage floor and the bandstand at Kristo's fell plaintively on Sam's ears.

There must have been a countdown, but he did not hear it. Suddenly the crisp clear notes of the bouzouki cascaded about the room. The strong bass strumming guitar and the drums counterpointing. Quickly.

"This is a syrtos from Crete," Kristo said. "My mother, when I was small, could dance this. She had tiny feet it seemed, and they moved like lightning, like something fast and delicate." He tapped his fingers on the table in time to the music.

The players looked calmly about, moving their hands swiftly, gracefully on the strings. Rapid sure notes.

"We danced, too, you know," Sam said, taking another sip of the coffee. "We have our dances, too, you know." He saw himself dressed white. He had danced with Thelma when they lived in Red Lodge. She wore a white dress with red roses embroidered around the neck. The music was like the music being played now. Yes, the band had played and they had danced until perspiration drenched them all. They were young and healthy and dark-headed. They clapped hands, danced in a circle, swept and bowed, stomped their feet and shouted, "Hey."

"Ay-la," said Kristo.

"Ay-la," answered the man with the guitar.

Sam tapped his foot.

"The Macedonians, some of them are Slavs, you know, you damned Greeks have half, Slavs have half. My father, he wasn't a dancer. He was a Montenegrin. Ornery son-of-a-bitch."

The young people of which Sam was one danced on the grass in the sunshine in a circle. The mountains were there in the distance, snowcapped peaks in summer. Sky brilliant blue, and there was a smell of flowers in the air. Red roses. Yugoslavs loved them. He should take some flowers to Thelma. But the perfume in his memory wasn't the scent of roses. He shook his head. Violets, yes. Deep and sweet and moist. Violets.

When he got home he would get some red roses for Thelma, and he would ask them in that florist's shop on the corner by the Dodge dealer if they had a bunch of violets. He would say to them, "No one wears violets anymore, no one. But I want a bunch of violets for my wife. She danced in a circle dressed in white, her hair was dark, her eyes were filled with love and music."

He saw her sitting in the bedroom, her back to him. He could not see her face. Her shoulders shook. Her eyes weren't filled with music, they were filled with tears. He had left the room.

The band finished the syrtos. The patrons applauded. The players smiled.

Sam said, "They bring back many memories."

Kristo nodded.

A young man in the back shouted, "Where is the belly dancer?" A ripple of laughter, the motion in the room.

"Later," said the man on the bandstand softly into

the microphone. He winked impersonally into the audience.

"Feeling better?" Kristo asked Sam.

"Yes," he answered. "The booze just got to me quicker than usual. Funny. I'm better now." He reached for the coffee cup again with a shaking hand.

It had been a bad day. He looked at his watch. Five minutes to twelve. Midnight and the birthday would be over. He thought he would be relieved, but a feeling of desperation encompassed him. Dread at the end of the ghostly day, yet an impulse to want it never to end. Close to something. That's what it was.

"Here's to a new day," he said to Kristo, lifting the coffee cup in a toast.

"We can all certainly use a new day," Kristo nodded and smiled. Shirl came into the room. She looked at Kristo, then at Sam. Without a gesture, she turned and left.

Sam had not seen her. He waited anxiously for the next song to begin.

"Shirl's back," Kristo said. "You want her to sit with us?"

Thelma, somewhere he could not reach. Shirl, somewhere he could not touch. Katy standing by the side of the road. He shook his head. He could not stand another face of accusation.

Katy saw Sam come in, but George did not. She nudged him and pointed. "Look, it's him."

"Terrific," said George. "Maybe he can throw us out of here, too."

Louie and Dinah slid into the booth with them.

"That's the guy that gave us the ride, so to speak," George said, nodding in the direction of Sam and Kristo.

"The dark-headed one, the one with the curly hair."

"That's Kristopoulis, the man who owns the place, with him," Louie said. As they all watched, Sam put the coffee cup to his lips.

"Well, there's the sweetheart of the Pizza Place." A loud voice caused all four of them to turn. The cowboy in the red shirt saluted them with a full glass of beer. He stood at the table. "Getting it on with somebody else, honey?" He grinned. He sloshed beer over the top of the glass and the liquid ran off the table into the lap of the cowboy in the blue shirt.

"You jackass," he said, brushing drops from his shirt and pants. "Sit down."

"No siree," said the cowboy in the red shirt. "Here's to you, baby." He pushed the glass forward and a stream of beer flew at the middle-aged couple at the table next to the boys. A plump woman wearing little bird earrings squealed. Her husband grunted something and got to his feet. Two large men appeared from the back of the room.

"Those jerks," Louie said.

"They're drunk as skunks," Dinah added.

The two burly men picked up the reveler and removed him, kicking and cursing, from the room.

Sam's face was turned directly toward them, but he gave no sign of recognition.

"He looks like a piss ant next to those bruisers," Louie said.

"That's what we need at the Pizza Place," Dinah said, lighting a cigarette. "A bouncer."

"Great idea," Louie agreed, and he blew out the match. "I think we ought to give the job to Katy here. Instead of throwing them out, she can kill them with a hot pizza."

"Katy's leaving for Berkeley tomorrow," George said. "She needs to get home."

Katy's mouth opened in surprise. "But . . ."

"If you don't have any money for the bus," George said, "I'll lend it to you."

"I thought you were going to stay," Dinah said.

"I wouldn't make much of a bouncer," Katy whispered.

Some people run away. Some people are sent. And from the darkness in their part of the room, Katy watched Sam. She squinted when the smoke from Dinah's cigarette curled in her eyes. George ordered another Black Russian, and Katy said she wanted one, too.

"The show will be starting soon," the waitress said. Her fine brown hair was teased into a high fluffy bonnet, and she wore backless pumps with tiny narrow heels. She walked quickly with her cork-topped tray, dipping in and out among the tables and the disorderly crowd.

The woman with the bird earrings complained loud enough for them all to hear.

"They should throw people like that out before they ruin someone's clothes," she insisted to her husband who listened patiently with the air of a man who was accustomed to such complaints.

"I mean, look at this." She pointed to a large wet spot on her breast. "This stain may not come out. We should talk to the management. They should never have let those cowboys in here in the first place." She set her jaw and all of her chins into lines of disapproval. She stretched to see over the crowd as if looking for someone to answer for the villainy.

"They threw him out, dear. What more can you expect?" Although the husband was not a small man, he appeared to be so next to the woman.

"You never," the woman said finally, "do what I want you to do."

The man shrugged and turned his chair so that he had his back to his wife and prepared to watch the show. Katy, her chin resting on her hand, stared at the booth where Sam and Kristopoulis sat.

"Come on," Louie said. "Bring on the dancing girl."

"Right," George said sullenly.

"What's the matter with you?" asked Louie.

"Nothing," said George.

Katy, who still watched Sam through the invisible tension, ignored Dinah's confused face and Louie's concern. Maybe she could ask Sam if she could ride with him tomorrow. If she could get the courage to go up to him.

The bouzouki player rippled up and down the scale. The drummer tested brushes on the small drums. The people in the club quieted. The music was about to begin. The men who played on the bandstand shifted on their feet, looked at one another, nodded and turned, in unison, full face to the audience, and the lights on their faces brightened, illuminating them at the exact moment when they began. Greek music poured out over the crowd, hushing and calming and thoroughly confusing the regular customers.

George tapped his feet to the rhythm. Dinah began to clap in time, and Louie shifted seductively and rapped his fingers on the table.

Katy kept time with her hand on her knee while her other hand caressed a place right in the middle of her stomach.

"Ay-la," a man yelled.

"Yasous," another man answered.

"Bring on the belly dancer," a young man called.

"Ay-laa," sang the guitar player, throwing back his head.

About the time when no one would have been able to stand further delay, the tempo of the music changed abruptly. The talk in the club ceased while the sultry strains of a tsifteteli signaled the approach of the belly dancer. The man who played the guitar stood at the microphone. He spoke in a deep voice, and he moved his dark eyes steadily around the room.

"Tonight, ladies and gentlemen, we have a special treat for you." He did not miss a note on the guitar as he spoke. The bouzouki player grinned at the drummer. "Direct from the island of Crete where she learned the art of belly dancing as it has existed since the gods of Olympus created the earth."

Sam blinked. Gods of Olympus created the earth. There was a small cluster of laughter. Of course, the myth, it was part of the show.

The tempo of the music increased. "Yes, the lady Magda is here tonight to demonstrate to you the beauty of this ancient dance. The subtle meanings of the birth of the universe are told in the many ways she moves her body."

"Sounds like a description of the hula," a woman seated at the table next to Sam said in a loud whisper. She raised her hand to smooth her hair and Sam noticed she wore a ring on each finger. "Isn't that what they always say in Hawaii, dear?" she cooed to a sour-looking man. "When can we go to Hawaii again, honey. This fall?" The man did not answer. Without taking his eyes from the guitar player, he reached for his Scotch and soda and took a long drink.

The man seemed cruel and cold to Sam. And just when he was feeling warm and comfortable again. He looked at his watch. Ten minutes past midnight. Yes, his birthday was over. The damned day had ended at last, and he waved to the waitress who passed by, and ordered a drink.

You ornery old bugger, he wanted to say to the man, but, of course, he would not. You with the shiny tan forehead and the greasy gray hair, he would say, you be nice to that lady. And he thought he saw Shirl again, standing in the doorway.

There was a sudden pause in the music and then it began again. It was louder now, the excitement building until, with a startling flourish from the drums, Magda came onto the dance floor. She swept into the center, her face partially covered by a veil, her green-shadowed eyes narrowed, her body hidden beneath layers of silk and chiffon. The coins jingled and rattled, and the crowd applauded and cheered. She whirled, the blue and green layers of cloth transparent as wings against the sun, the coins cold hard gold in contrast. Sam, too, clapped his hands in time to the music. He felt a rush of affection for the dancer, for the pleasure she was giving. He moved his fingers across the black plastic table top, feeling the shiny oily surface.

"Something, hey, Sam?" Kristo leaned into his face, whispered with a hot breath smelling of garlic and cigar smoke. "Even in Winnemucca?"

"You old devil," Sam nudged him.

Magda jingled and jangled by their table. She winked at Sam, and he winked back at her. She glittered and she held her veil away from her body, turning, hiding herself again while the hard knock steady beat of the drum kept the rhythm and the bouzouki and guitar rose and fell, faster, slower, all around. Her finger cymbals held high above her head, flashed in the lights. Bare braceleted feet, pale running, grinding steps, and her green-shadowed eyes picked and chose among the men in the audience. Her hips were slipping round and snapping to the rhythm, catching the down beat, whirling on the up. Everyone moved in some way, with her, with a part of the body, of the soul.

"Ay-la," cried the guitar player.

"Yasous," shouted the drummer.

"Ah, Fatima," sighed the bouzouki man.

"Eh, eh, eh," called a man from across the floor, a short man with dark shiny hair and a patch over one eye.

"There's old Nick Paulos," Kristo whispered to Sam. "Crazy old Greek. I called him specially for tonight. He'll dance, himself, you see."

"Eh, eh, eh," the man shouted again, and pounded the table in time to the music and the dancing Magda.

"He couldn't get used to the glass eye. That's why he wears the patch," Kristo said.

The man waved at Kristo as if he heard himself being explained. He raised a hand and signaled okay with a circle made from his thumb and index finger. Then he went back to hammering the table with his fist, steadily, precisely, in the right time.

"We have music in our blood, my brother," Kristo said.

And Kristo was right. That was it. He wasn't missing a step himself. Warm and safe. All the blood and bone had returned to his hands. To his body. He could feel the table, his feet on the floor. Shirl? That was a mistake. Gone with the past and the death of his birthday.

Everything went with the show, with the woman who now tossed aside one veil revealing her navel and the blue jewel that glistened there.

And it seemed to Sam as if there were stars twinkling everywhere, from the catching and tossing back of the spotlights that picked out silver studs on the instruments, to the fascinating blue jewel in the center of the dancer. The music increased, the dancer whirled, billowing veils like evening storm clouds, blue against the sky. Faster. The man with the patch over his eye kept perfect time with his fist. The customers did not talk; they watched and Magda met their eyes, tossed her head, and let her long black hair pour down her back. With her hands she urged the audience on, clapping the finger cymbals, reaching, begging, grasping for attention.

And when it seemed impossible for the dance to continue, the musicians with a stunning crescendo, finished with three powerful chords, and Magda bowed to the floor.

The scattering of applause was cut short. The dance was not over. The musicians began a slow, sensuous melody and sent it pulsing into the room. The lights in the club changed to red, and the people strained to see the dancer on the floor. Her knees were bent underneath her, and she leaned back until she touched the floor with her hair. Arms, now red, rose slowly over her body, slipping into the air like angular snakes, beckoning to the gods, no longer tempting in the level direction of man.

"The birth of the world," Kristo said in a whisper. "See how she seems to have something alive, something circling in her belly?"

Sam could not take his eyes from the seemingless headless and legless dancer. It was as if something lived within the flesh, as if something writhed and struggled to be free. The life inside circled the blue jewel and in the center of the jewel, a white star blinded Sam. A feeling not unlike pain coursed along the surface of his arms and legs just under the skin, making him shiver as he watched. The red light made it difficult to see. The jewel was no longer blue, but a dark gleaming purple. Her skin was red, alive and moving.

"This will be a better day, Sam," Kristo said. "You'll see."

Sam felt his breath shorten, his heart begin to pound. Something was happening to him. He was cold in the red light, the music seemed to fill his head and flow across his eyes, and he could not see. He tightened his fist and felt the pressure continue to build in his head. What was happening to him? Was the music louder now? It was so slow, so endless. Like the tone in his head. Yes, that was it. Like that shrill note. And in that undulating belly (that was all he could see) was a growth, a roundness that moved and lived. Like a tumor. He shook his head. The light made him dizzy; the music was now unbearable. He thought he might have to leave. He looked desperately at Kristo, and he was unable to focus on the man's face. What was it he dreaded? He placed his hand to his throat to stop the pounding of the blood.

He was waiting for a scream. That was it. A scream, an agonizing pain-filled piercing scream. A birth scream, a death scream, anything loud enough to let him go.

Please, he wanted to shout, *please let go. Scream.*

And the dancer, like a sultry red ghost was rising from the floor. First her arms, the arching of the back, the hands still pulling at the deity in the sky, still caressing the fiery tails of comets as they slipped through her fingers, trailing red and evaporating in her grasp. Orion's daughters, escaping. Sam's face was on fire, sweat ran down his cheeks. The dancer rose higher, pulling her hair up and off the floor. Slowly she penetrated the sky, standing, moving, the music dragged up with her. Sam thought he would have to scream himself. A death cry, yes. He felt it building, rising through his body, filling his lungs.

But the voice he wanted to hear was not his own, but Julianna's.

And then the lights were up, the dancer blue and green and gold and fast, the music back to the quick tsifteteli. The coins rattled and the red was gone. Magda looked at Sam and narrowed the green-shadowed eyes and it was as if the birth was a dream, a false alarm, the red light a mirage, the scream, a laugh, and everything but the pounding in his throat, a misunderstanding. People applauded and cheered. There was foot stomping, and finger snapping. Whistling. Magda moved among the tables. Dollar bills appeared in shaky hands. An old man grinned toothlessly and stuck a dollar in her belt. The woman with the little bird earrings frowned and handed her husband a dollar from her purse, then looked the other way.

The unuttered scream was broken into sharp pieces in Sam's throat. He gasped for breath, and Kristo looked with concern.

"Are you all right?" he asked.

Sam tried to smile. A feeble nod. How could he wait for words from a dead child, for a scream from the grave?

"She's good, isn't she?" Kristo asked. "What do you think, Sam Batinovich?"

"Yes," the words were released by Sam's brain, and he was surprised at the calm sound. "That's some show all right. Some dance."

He could hear Magda moving about, laughter here and there. He knew Kristo watched her closely, but Sam had difficulty focusing. Magda danced back onto the floor, did a final spin with her veils, and with a resolute one, two, three from the bouzouki, stopped, bowed, and ran from the floor.

The applause was enthusiastic and harsh to Sam's ears. He signaled to the waitress. She came to the table, scowling on the way at the sour-faced man who still sat half turned away from his wife who continued to smooth her hair with both hands and a total of ten rings on her fingers.

Rings on her fingers bells on her toes,/And she shall have music wherever she goes. Julianna, her hands folded in front of her, wide-eyed, three years old. *Ride a cockhorse to Banbury Cross, /To see a fine lady upon a white horse.*

Sam smiled. He saw Magda, with blue and green veils and golden coins, astride the white horse. Magda with the long dark hair. Plump like the horse that reared back on its heels, nostrils flaring. *Rings on her fingers* . . .

The waitress repeated her question. "What can I get you?"

Kristo looked at Sam. "Wait," the Greek said. "Bring a bottle of ouzo from my stock upstairs." He grinned at Sam. "Ouzo and two shot glasses."

At first she looked suspicious, then she smiled. "Celebration, huh?"

And Kristo said, "Give a bottle to the man over there with the eye patch. To him and to his friends."

She turned to go. Sam could not find the words to stop her, though he wasn't sure why he should want to. The musicians began to play again, and Sam leaned back in the booth and tried to think.

In the back of the room, Katy Daniels and her friends whispered. George and Dinah and Louie had stood to see the dancer as she lay on the floor. Katy stayed seated at the table and touched the pain in her stomach.

"Do you see him?" George asked.

"He's still there," Katy replied.

"You can never tell what a crazy man will do," George said.

"At least he didn't cut your arm off and leave you in the desert," Louie laughed.

"You wouldn't think it was so funny if your name was George instead of Louie," George said.

"Hey, listen, only kidding, man."

George frowned. "Just my luck to be named after a one-armed corpse."

"You guys are sick," said Dinah.

"Speaking of only one of something, there's old man Paulos, the guy with the eye patch," Louie said. "His son owns a whole chain of laundromats in California. Old man talks about him all the time."

"What happened to his eye?" Katy asked.

"A rock flew up from his power mower," Dinah said.

"It's not as dramatic as having your arm chopped off," Louie said.

"Get off it," Dinah shuddered. "You give me the creeps."

"And it was his birthday, too," Katy said. She was greeted with blank stares from Dinah and Louie. "Sam's," she said. "Mr. Batinovich. His daughter had died and it was his birthday."

The waitress put a bottle of clear liquor in front of Sam and Kristopoulis, then took another bottle to the man with the eye patch. Sam and Kristo raised small glasses to toast the one-eyed man. He raised his glass in return. Then he put the glass between his teeth, dropped his hands to the table, dipped his head back, drinking the shot at once.

The people close around him applauded. The bouzouki player bowed. The guitar player struck the down chord and the music began. Mr. Paulos, with his bottle in one hand, the glass in the other, stepped to the center of the floor.

"You don't want me to stay here," Katy whispered to George, "do you?"

"No," he said.

"Zeimbekiko," Kristo said to Sam and placed a comforting hand on his shoulder. "A dance to represent the unshed tears of a man's life."

Paulos set the glass and the bottle in the middle of the floor. He put his arms out like the wings of a bird and began to sway to the heavy slow beat of the music. He snapped his fingers and moved in a circle around the bottle of ouzo. He projected and extended his legs, slapped his heels hard, closed his eye, and concentrated on the balance. He jumped into the air; he knelt on the floor. He slapped the hard wood with his palm, then balanced on that hand.

He flirted with the glass of ouzo, teased it, dipped close to it, then drew away as if the glass held a peril and yet was irresistible. The Sirens singing sweetly in a meadow, surrounded by the bones of men.

Sam clapped large unfeeling hands with a slow even pulse. He watched, astonished at the dexterity of the man. Paulos arched his back, bending nearly to the floor. The crowd clapped, louder, harder. Sam began to feel his hands stinging together as he dared the man to pick up the glass, to listen to the Siren's song.

Paulos held his arms out straight, his knees nearly touched the floor. He had the glass in his teeth. He began slowly to rise to the standing position. He balanced. The audience cheered. He kept his eyes fixed on the glass. And then, with a sudden sharp movement, he flipped his head back and downed the glass of ouzo.

Cheers, bows. Paulos' friends threw dollar bills onto the floor.

"You should have been a Greek," Kristo said, smiling. He lit his damp cigar. "Ah, Sam, to be Greek."

"You think a Slav can't do that, hey?" Sam said. "You think you Greeks are the only ones who can dance?"

His voice seemed extraordinarily loud.

"Listen, old man, I've done some dancing, too, you know."

Thelma in a white dress, dark pretty eyes. No. A line of men in white pants and shirts. Red and black sashes.

He picked up the glass of ouzo in his teeth and tried the stunt. Two tiny trickles rolled down the corners of his mouth.

"Not bad," Kristo laughed, "for a Slav."

Sam filled the glass again. This time, he got almost all of the liquid in his mouth. It burned down the back of his throat, the licorice flavor overwhelming but welcome. By the third glass, Sam had almost mastered the trick. He clapped Kristo on the shoulder. "Even an old dog," he said.

"You're stealing my stuff," Paulos said, and he slammed his fist in mock anger on the table.

Kristo introduced them. The man's handshake was tough and sinewy. Sam nodded to him.

"They're going to do a tsamiko," Paulos said, "Come on, you old Greek." He pulled a white kerchief from his pocket.

"You tell them *slow*," Kristo ordered. He turned to Sam. "You say you dance? We'll see. Tsamiko. Yasous."

Sam thought he caught a glimpse of Shirl in the corner of the room at the door by the cashier. You shouldn't have left me there, she would say to him. You shouldn't run away like that. He felt the flush of guilt. He gripped the edge of the table to steady himself. Paulos stood in the middle of the floor, his arm raised, the white silk kerchief hanging. Kristo, head held high, back straight, reached for the tail of the kerchief. Someone applauded; Kristo smiled and bowed, then snapped his fingers at the band and extended his arm for Sam.

The light on the floor seemed uncommonly bright. The hardwood gleamed gold and nearly blinded Sam. He put his hand on Kristo's shoulder and the two elbows locked and formed a strong bond between the two men. Sam held his left hand behind his back. The music began and he closed his eyes for a moment to remember, to feel the rhythm. He prayed he would not fall down. When he opened his eyes, the audience had faded into darkness, and it was as if the dancers were at the center of the sun. The music was faster than he remembered, but they formed a strong line. Straight, locked together. Paulos began. Step, cross, step, cross, yes. Sam could remember. He snapped his fingers behind his back. Snap, click, click, snap. Four steps, eight beats forward. Two steps, four beats back. They progressed, the line of men. Evenly, proudly. Yes, that was it, Sam thought. Head high, back straight. The hero, the warrior, the dancer. The men were all alone. They faced straight forward, and moved smoothly sideways. Heavy step, light ones, heavy step.

Then Paulos began the acrobatics. Kristo braced himself, and the smaller man, with one eye, twisted and leapt to the music. He was suspended there, slapping his heels.

The line moved forward. Sam knew he was there, watching, cheering, holding the end of the line, but the distance was increasing. He saw the face of his father. Words of stories came to his mind.

He lost the step for a moment, missed a beat. He nearly stumbled. Instead, he grunted apologetically and tried to concentrate. The folk tales, the myths. His father talking of the mountains, looking down to the passes where the young men marched to the sea. The boys of Serbia marched, leaving death and disease, until they fell mad into the sea at Corfu. Had his father marched, too? Was that his father's madness? Had he been lured from the herds of the mountain tops by the steadily moving line of men, the same way Sam was lured by the dance?

No one knew. His father fell silent when the subject was approached. Yugoslavs watched his face, leaned forward, looking for a clue in the black eyes.

"I," he would say, "am a Montenegrin. I look down from the cliffs. I tended my sheep and looked down."

The music moved about Sam and the other men. The

people in the room seemed to have disappeared. But they were there, in the dark, secretly watching. Yes, like his father had done while all those young men marched starving through the valleys of his country. They marched in the light paths, trailed the river, died and fell into the water, killing the others that came later along the path and drank from the streams filled with bloated bodies.

And Sam, his head high, his back straight, his feet locked into the rhythm, paced with the pattern of the dance, while Paulos leapt and slapped his heels, his one eye looking heavenward.

And Sam knew his father had marched with those boys to the sea. At last he understood the black look in his father's eyes. He had marched, no question. Pulled along by a line of movement, the way Sam was pulled along, the reflection of death in his glance.

Kristo shouted, "Ay-la."

Paulos leapt into the air, and with a flourish the music ended. The men clapped each other on the shoulders.

"It's been years," Kristo said, "since a tsamiko." He panted, his hand to his chest. "Old man, out of breath." Ah, but the spark was in his eyes. "I'm going to Greece, you know, Paulos, soon. It's good I should practice."

"Ouzo," Paulos held out his hand to receive a shot glass of the liquor. "Ah, it inspires, it is life."

Sam too, was breathing heavily, and the perspiration was cold on his forehead. He reached in his pocket for his handkerchief and discovered he did not have one. Paulos wiped his own perspiring brow with white silk. The eye patch looked even blacker in contrast.

"And you thought a Slav couldn't keep up with you, eh?" Sam said.

"You want to lead the next one?" Kristo winked at him. "You want to leap in the air like that, like Paulos here?" He laughed loudly, and Sam joined in.

Then, suddenly, he was sick, nausea welling from his stomach into his throat. He had to get out of the room. He looked blindly at Kristo, saw the light in the room darken around the edges of his vision. He put his hand out and Kristo slowly turned his back. He did not see Sam.

The sickness pulled at him, the terrible bubbling after-taste of the ouzo warning him. He was dizzy, and the darkness obliterated the people. At the back of the room, a square of light at the door beckoned. He lurched forward, swallowing, widening his eyes, staring at the light. He moved through the crowd. He did not see the faces; he heard voices but did not understand the words. If he could get outside, if he could fall into the dark of the night with the stars and cool air, he could fall into the grass, sink into the earth. The ouzo, the embarrassment, the failure.

A woman with a straw purse decorated with shells cursed him. "Watch out," she said, grabbing her handbag.

"Drunk," said a man who knew.

"He was the one who was dancing," whispered the lady with the earrings shaped like birds.

He bumped against a table, and a young man with a black mustache said, "Shit, you spilled my drink, man." Sam tried to find his face, and could not. At the square of light, Shirl stepped forward, reached for his arm. He pushed her away without regard for her concern. In the lobby, for a moment, he was totally blinded. Then, seeing the exit, he pushed at the glass doors. God, he hoped he wouldn't fall through them, fall shattering the glass. He could feel the piercing pain of laceration, slivers of glass in his arms and his face, but he was through the door out onto the sidewalk. He turned toward his motel; the street was fading in the distance. He saw the flickering neon lights of the Star Broiler and Casino. Something was locked in his head, and it was blacking out his sight. He leaned back against the building. He could feel the rough brick. He felt the edges scrape his back like finger-nails as he began to slip. He swallowed desperately, forcing the nausea down and away with sheer will.

The white lights from the Star Broiler took over what remained of his vision, filling crevasses and then were extinguished.

There was a hand on his arm, a voice from long ago and far away in his ear.

"Come on," she said. "Let me help you," she whispered.

He put his hand in front of him like a blind man.

"I can't see," he whimpered.

"Sit down," she led him. "Here, sit down."

He heard the voice through a roar of bird wings beat-ing close around his head. He moved on legs made of stone, following the voice, the cool hand on his arm. He didn't know how far they walked. He thought he leaned on a mirage, that he would open his eyes, and find that nothing supported him, and he would collapse, but he could feel the hand, steady and cool.

"Come on."

He did not know how long he had been unable to see, how far they had walked, or where they were. When his vision returned, he saw the silhouette of a tree, leaves dark against the moonlit sky. He sat on a bench and he was calm, the cold sweat drying on his face. The pain in his head was gone. He put one hand in his pocket and sat like an ordinary man who took midnight walks, who sat in the park and looked at the stars on a summer evening.

"Here," she said, and he saw a paper cup filled with water.

He looked up into her face as he took the cup and tears welled in his eyes. It was the girl, Katy. He thought he would see Julianna standing there. He would hear her say, "Here, Daddy, have a drink of water, you'll feel better."

"Are you okay, now?" she asked. She sat down next to him on the bench.

The water was lukewarm and tasted of chlorine. He grimaced.

"I know that water's no good. I tasted it," she said, "but it's better than nothing."

He was confused. He looked about the park, blinking away the tears.

"I got it at the service station, the one there," she said.

Sam saw the red, white, and blue neon stripes of a Standard station on the corner. Nevada stations, open all night. What time was it? Why was the girl with him again? Had she ever been gone?

"Thanks," he murmured.

"I liked watching you dance," she said.

"I've had too much ouzo," he replied, closing his eyes against another whirl of vision. "Kristo, my friend, he's the Greek and he—I drank too much." He moved his hand to his head. Still no pain. He was only tired.

"Would you like to go home?" she asked. "I'll walk with you."

Sam felt the tears run at his eyes again. He nodded, then spoke. "I need to go home."

She got up from the bench and looked at him. "Come on, then," she said softly.

When he stood, he noticed for the first time how small she was, and when she gazed up at him, her face expressionless, her eyes were dark in the moonlight. They began the walk to his motel. She was close to him, and he reached out and put his arm around her shoulders. She was delicate, her skin smooth. He rubbed his hand on her pale shoulder as if to warm her.

She slipped her arm around his waist and they walked, like old friends about to fall in love, down the cracked sidewalk in Winnemucca, Nevada.

And the show at Kristo's was over. Magda folded the blue silk veil and placed it on top of the others. She snapped the suitcase shut. Kristo waited for her, his keys in his hand.

He thought he heard her whisper, "Daddy, I love you," while he made love to her, but he knew it was an illusion. Though it sounded real, it was merely a wish.

And it was as though every moment of tenderness in Sam's life crystallized at the tips of his fingers when he touched her. He lay next to her in the bed, smoothing her hair away from her face, kissing the cut on her forehead, tracing her lips with his finger. He toyed with the tiny silver stars that dangled from her ear lobes. When she put her arms around him and held him, he wanted to weep with the warmth of it all.

And when she moved passionately with him, he wanted to consume her, keep her, lock her in the center of his soul and in his body, forever. Delicate arms, hair fine against his face, and never had he been so gentle and so aware.

Later, while she slept, he sat in the chair in front of the window and stared out at the night. He had opened the drapes enough to see the pool and the light that reflected there. The bannisters were white in the moonlight, the doors to the rooms, dark blue. He thought about people sleeping there. He wondered where they were going, and what they whispered to each other in the middle of the night. He smoked cigarette after cigarette, feeling the smoke fill his lungs. He thought of Thelma, and he was anxious to see her. A desire to touch her, to tell her he was sorry for all the years he had not understood, had not touched her with his whole heart, consumed him. He thought of how completely he had loved Julianna, and while he watched the smoke curl in the moonlight, he hoped she was not alone, that Thelma was not alone. He looked protectively at the girl in the bed. She moaned lightly once or twice, and he wondered what dreams moved in her head, what visions passed before her eyes.

He did not know how long he sat by the window. The sky was taking on the lighter cast when he stood from the chair. The three stars of Orion's girdle were just visible on the horizon, his chase nearly ended for the night. He, too, could rest.

He walked over to the bed and looked down at the sleeping girl. She was so still she could have been dead. Her face was calm in the middle of the pillow, and she was completely motionless. Sam watched for the movement of her breathing and could not detect it. She was small, fragile, her expression peaceful. Did she look like Julianna or was it the blurring of his vision again? If Julianna had died before her body shriveled and her hair fell out, she would have looked like this princess, frozen in sleep.

It was almost dawn. The room was lighter, with a blue cast to it all. He wanted to lie by her side, to touch the curves of her body once more. He sat carefully on the edge of the bed. He did not want to wake her. He pulled the sheet away from her to see her body in the softening night.

At first, he thought he had lost his mind, that he must be hallucinating. The stain, dark and murky, grew in a circle about the girl's hips. Maroon, purple, black, spreading, and he had to touch it before he could accept the fact of the blood.

He knew there was too much of it. The words circled in his mind. *Too much blood*. He was paralyzed at the sight. He thought she was dead. The circle widening, then seeming to pulse under his flickering vision. Her body was white on top of the stain, and she did not move. Words caught and cracked in his throat. When he reached out to touch her face, he was terrified.

She moaned and her eyes fluttered open. He leaned close to her, unable to believe she was alive. He stared at the blood on his hand.

"What's wrong?" she asked softly, looking into his eyes.

And before him, he saw the horror shatter the innocence in her face. Her lips parted; she struggled to sit up. She drew her hand up to her eyes and saw the red smear.

"I'm pregnant," she said, staring at her hand.

"Lie down and don't move," Sam ordered. He stood and rushed to dress. He heard her crying, short soft cries. She was afraid, he could hear it.

"It'll be all right," he said. "Don't worry, I'll get you to the hospital."

"My stomach hurts," she groaned. And when he turned she was still lying on her back in the pool of blood, her hands pressed to her belly, her small breasts trembling.

He pulled on his shoes. He would wrap her in the bedspread, yes, carry her to the car. Hospital. Yellow brick building. Where was it exactly . . . two streets down, on a side street, a sign with white letters. HOSPITAL.

She covered her face with her hands and sobbed. Sam leaned over her, lifting her gently and placing her on the bedspread. The blood was scarcely visible against the dark blue cloth, but he could see it flowing from her, and he hurried to wrap the spread around her. She saw the stain and hid her face again.

"Oh," she moaned. "Oh no."

He searched for his keys, saw them lying on the dresser and snatched them up. Hospital.

"It will be all right. Nothing to worry about." He thought to open the door, to unlock the station wagon before he picked her up to leave.

In the early morning light, the sky to the east, pink, he placed the bleeding girl in the front seat. A yellow brick building a few blocks away.

A man stood in front of the window of his room. He held the white drape to the side, and he watched from the second story of the motel as the man carried the girl wrapped in a blue bedspread to the station wagon. The man who watched was shirtless, and wore slacks without a belt. His briefcase sat, unopened on the chair by the window. He watched as the station wagon backed out of the place, and he heard the tires screech as the man drove out onto the street.

"What happened?" Shirl asked from the bed. "What are you looking at?" The sheet was pulled up to her chin.

"It's almost morning," the man said as he turned to her. He unfastened the top of his slacks and walked to the bed.

Alone in the corridor, Sam walked with quiet steps. He paced, hands folded behind his back, head down. Occasionally, he stopped and looked at a picture on the wall. This hospital had French street scenes hanging on the pale green walls. There wasn't a single sunflower.

He glanced often to the door marked EMERGENCY, and he wondered what the white-gowned phantoms were doing to Katy. He waited for a doctor to come out through that door and explain to him exactly what was the matter, as if he had a right to know.

He sat down on a brown leather couch and lit a cigarette. He was alone.

"Miscarriage," the young doctor with the wire-rimmed glasses had mumbled. "Don't worry."

Sam smiled, irony echoing.

A life had ended, a life carried inside Katy, and the doctor said, "Don't worry." Right. What was there to worry about? *No more dying then.* A line from a poem. Something. He could not remember. *Death once dead, there's no more dying then.* It didn't make sense to him. Had someone said it at Julianna's funeral? He could not recall. A coffin covered with red roses and white gardenias. Sitting in the aisle of the church. He had not taken his eyes off the casket during the entire service. He did not remember the music.

A hospital waiting room. How many hours, weeks, days. He looked around dispassionately. It was familiar, the feeling, one of contempt for the surroundings. But the fear was gone, though he could not define the difference in the way he felt.

"Are you the girl's husband?" a nurse appeared in front of him.

"No. I'm just a friend," Sam replied, standing from the couch. "I brought her in." He extinguished the cigarette in the ashtray next to the couch.

"Is there family we should notify?" the nurse asked.

A spasm of fright made Sam clench his fists. *Notify. You should notify any other close relatives. The time is near . . .*

"What's happened?" He tried to control his rising anger. "Where is she?"

"She'll be all right," the nurse said, and she looked at the wide-banded watch on her wrist. "They will be putting her in a room in a few minutes. You can see her then."

"Why should anyone be notified?" Sam wanted the nurse to look him in the eye. She seemed uncomfortable. Something must be wrong.

"It's a matter of the bill, things like that. Releases." The words trailed off. The nurse was embarrassed.

"I'll pay the bill before I leave," Sam said.

"The doctor will talk to you," she said, and she turned down the corridor. The familiar sound of her rubber-soled shoes squeaking against the tile drove Sam to reach for another cigarette. When he got home, he would have to give it up all over again. The smoking. He lit the cigarette with a packet of matches from Johnny Leone's Restaurant in Elko, Nevada. *Call us for reservations.*

He wondered what had happened to Johnny's nephew.

He thought about Cora and the jokes. *Once there was an Italian wrestler named Giuseppe* . . . Cora with the ruffled handkerchief with the flowers sewn in the corner. The sweet heavy smell of violets, and Joy perfume.

He should try to call Thelma again. He looked at his watch. Six-thirty. He was six and one half hours into his forty-second year. He stood and walked to the window.

The sun was bright in Winnemucca. The sound of traffic along the main street was muffled by the heavy glass, but when he parted the blinds he could see the summer caravan was already moving. Big cars pulling trailers. Volkswagen buses. Small cars with luggage racks on the top looking strangely human. They all crept along through the town.

He looked down the side street, the row of white frame houses. A woman in a housecoat watered the marigolds in front of her porch. A boy on a bicycle steered with one hand and threw newspapers in the general direction of front doors as he rode.

It was going to be a damned hot day and the air conditioner was broken in the wagon. He had customers in Reno, and he was tired. He rubbed at his chin. He needed a shave and the roughness reminded him of Katy's smooth skin, of her hair, of the tiny star earrings. He had a terrible taste in his mouth, and he walked down the hall, hoping to see a vending machine of some kind. Coffee, gum, a candy bar, anything.

He walked to the end of the corridor. In an alcove was a soft drink machine. He searched his pockets for change. A root beer.

Julianna loved root beer floats. He never saw a can of root beer but that he remembered her glass stuffed with ice cream, flooded with root beer, topped with foam. She spooned the foam off first, then mixed the ice cream with the root beer, pulling on the straw.

Root beer floats and charcoal broiled hamburgers with a big slice of purple onion. When he got home, he would set up the barbecue. He and Thelma would sit out on the patio and have a drink. They would sit on that redwood furniture that had been covered with plastic for the past three months, and they would talk. They would invite the neighbors over, and they would laugh. He would cook hamburgers and mix bourbon and sodas for everyone. And Thelma could wear the Joy perfume that he would buy her as soon as he got home.

He had just tossed the empty root beer can into the wastebasket when the nurse summoned him.

"You can see her now," she said, indicating to him that she gave her permission with reservation. "Follow me."

Katy looked pale and sleepy, but she smiled at Sam. An intravenous was set up next to her bed, and the memory of the clear liquid that had dropped into Julianna's veins startled Sam, then he shook the thought away.

At the same instant, both Katy and Sam turned to see the woman in the next bed. Katy attempted to sit up, to get a better look. Sam blinked, trying to remember the face.

The woman's head was wrapped in bandages, and she was motionless on the pillow, her mouth set in a line, her breathing barely detectable. The nurse, seeing Sam and Katy staring, moved and pulled a curtain between the beds.

"She's unconscious," the nurse said.

"What happened to her?" Katy asked while Sam still tried to remember where he had seen the woman.

"It's a real sad case," the nurse said, putting her hands in the pockets of her uniform. "She and her family were in an accident. Her husband and little girl were killed outright, but she was thrown clear. She hasn't regained consciousness yet."

"Husband and little girl?" Katy repeated, her eyes widening, her hand pulling at the pink spread.

"Yes. Brought them in around six last night. The driver, the husband I guess, must have run right into the back of that camper," she shook her head.

Sam reached for Katy's desperate hand. What was wrong with her? The nurse spoke matter of factly as if she had told the story many times.

"Was it a blue car?" Katy asked.

"I wouldn't know about that. Do you know her?"

Katy closed her eyes. "No," she whispered. "I don't know her."

"It's going to be terrible when she wakes up," the nurse said.

The doctor with the wire-rimmed glasses entered the room.

"What happened to the people in the camper?" Katy asked.

"Oh, they were banged up some," the nurse replied. She looked at the doctor. "They're all right."

Katy's hand was cold in Sam's, but still.

"Well, everything looks fine," the doctor said. "Lost some blood but we gave her a transfusion. Should be all right. She should stay overnight, then she can go in the morning."

The man and the woman in the blue car, the little girl with the sunsuit. The man, standing in front of the desert sun. Offering to help. Angering Sam. Why had he been so angry? And now, the man dead, the child dead. The mother motionless behind the pink curtain of the hospital room.

And Sam looked directly at the doctor and asked the question.

"What caused the miscarriage?" He felt the heat of the blood rushing to his face. He gripped Katy's hand, and she squeezed his in return.

"It was a spontaneous abort," the doctor said. "Malformed fetus. A blessing, really. Better to happen now than later."

The words were so cold. The doctor even smiled at the end of the sentence. "Lucky someone was with her."

"Yes," she whispered and closed her eyes.

She looked so damned tired, Sam thought. Weak, and tired. But there was the smallest blush of color on her cheeks.

"She'll go to sleep pretty soon," the doctor said. "Will you check at the desk before you leave the hospital this morning?" he said politely.

Sam nodded.

Soundlessly, white and crisp, the doctor and nurse left the room.

"They gave us a ride," Katy said without opening her eyes. "The man and the woman and the little girl. That woman over there."

"Yes," said Sam.

"They let us out in Winnemucca."

"Don't think about them now," he whispered. "Don't get more upset."

"I didn't want that baby," Katy said.

Sam nodded silently. He saw tiny tears in the corners of Katy's eyes. He wanted to brush her hair back from her forehead once again, and tell her everything was all right now. The stars dangled against the pillow.

"Do you want me to call your parents now?" Sam asked. He held her hand and stroked the back of it, tracing the pattern of veins.

"No," she said.

"But they should be told." He covered her hand with his.

"Couldn't you just take me home tomorrow? I could tell them, I promise I will tell them . . ." The tears were larger now and rolled down her cheeks.

"Sure," Sam said. "I can wait for you a day."

"I'm sorry for all the trouble," she said.

"I know."

"I thought I was going to die," Katy said with her eyes still closed. "It was the oddest feeling."

He sat holding her hand until she went to sleep. He stared at the drawn pink curtain and listened to the sound of her breathing. He could hear occasional noises from the street, but the woman on the other side of the curtain was deathly silent. He wondered who was the father of Katy's lost child, but could not concentrate hard enough to conjure up an image.

She looked like a little girl, untouched, lying in the bed. She had lost a baby she did not want and somewhere a father had lost a child, and he would never know.

When Sam entered the corridor, the nurse smiled sympathetically at him. He looked at his watch. Nine-thirty in the morning. Twenty-four hours since he first saw Katy and his own reflection in her glasses.

"Is there a pay phone somewhere on this floor?" he asked the nurse.

She pointed to the far end of the hall. "Right around the corner," she said.

He dialed the number, the operator intercepted, he deposited the coins, and he listened to the ringing.

On the fourth ring, Thelma answered.

"I had to stay with the Tomichs' little boy while they took their daughter for an appendectomy," she said. "I hope you weren't too worried."

"I'll be a full day late," Sam said. "It'll be late tomorrow night. The air conditioner broke; I spent longer in Winnemucca than I planned."

"I've missed you, Sam," she said.

"I'll be glad to get home." He felt his hand tighten on the receiver and the tears come to his eyes.

"Sam?" she said in the distance. "I almost forgot."

"What?" The word nearly choked him.

"Happy Birthday."